UNDER HIS
PROTECTION

RED STONE SECURITY SERIES

Katie Reus

Cover art: Jaycee of Sweet 'N Spicy Designs
JRT Editing
Author website: http://www.katiereus.com

Under His Protection/Katie Reus. -- 1st ed.

ISBN-13: 978-1500612962
ISBN-10: 1500612960

eISBN: 9780996087438

For my wonderful readers.

Praise for the novels of Katie Reus

"…an engrossing page-turner that I enjoyed in one sitting. Reus offers all the ingredients I love in a paranormal romance." —Book Lovers, Inc.

"Has all the right ingredients: a hot couple, evil villains, and a killer action-filled plot. . . . [The] Moon Shifter series is what I call Grade-A entertainment!" —Joyfully Reviewed

"I could not put this book down. . . . Let me be clear that I am not saying that this was a good book *for* a paranormal genre; it was an excellent romance read, *period.*" —All About Romance

"Reus strikes just the right balance of steamy sexual tension and nail-biting action….This romantic thriller reliably hits every note that fans of the genre will expect." —*Publisher's Weekly*

"Prepare yourself for the start of a great new series! . . . I'm excited about reading more about this great group of characters." —Fresh Fiction

"Nonstop action, a solid plot, good pacing and riveting suspense…" —*RT Book Reviews (4.5 Stars)*

"Wow! This powerful, passionate hero sizzles with sheer deliciousness. I loved every sexy twist of this fun & exhilarating tale. Katie Reus delivers!" —Carolyn Crane, author of *Into the Shadows*

Continued…

CHAPTER ONE

Julieta Mederos looked up from her computer screen as the bell above her shop door jingled. She inwardly cringed. She thought she'd locked the door. It was ten minutes until closing but as the owner of Julieta's Silk and Lace she could make executive decisions. And it was Friday night, she was starving, and the employee she'd had scheduled to close this evening had called in sick. Again.

Since no one else had been able to come in, she'd been stuck covering. *Again.* She hated to let anyone go, but tomorrow morning she was making the call.

Shoving those thoughts away she smiled at the beautiful couple entering. "Hi, please feel free to shop around and let me know if you have any questions about anything."

The woman was tall, slender and wearing a long, bright print Bohemian-style dress with simple gold sandals. She was truly stunning, the kind of woman Julieta wouldn't be surprised to see gracing the cover of a magazine. She smiled back, her expression tentative. "I saw the hours on your door, are you sure you're still open?" When she fingered the strap of her purse, the giant diamond on her left hand, ring finger glinted under the colorful track lighting.

Julieta nodded, already liking the woman from that one thoughtful question. "I'm Julieta so I can stay open as late as you'd like." She flicked a glance to the tall, blond man standing next to her. He looked like a sexy Viking god. Well, a sexy, angry one. He was practically glaring at her. *Okay then.*

Maybe Julieta's discomfort showed on her face because the woman nudged the male in the sharp black suit next to her. "I'm going to shop and my friend here is going to sit right over there." There was an edge to her voice as the woman pointed to a plush couch next to a glass-cased display of discreet sex toys.

Practically growling, the man went to stand next to the couch, turning his body so that he had a view of the front door and the rest of the shop. As Julieta watched him she realized just how huge he was. Most people were taller than her anyway, but with broad shoulders and a muscular body even a suit couldn't hide, a sliver of anxiety threaded through her veins. She'd never been robbed before, but she wasn't stupid enough to think it couldn't happen to her.

Julieta sold high-end lingerie, but she also sold affordable, quality fashion jewelry and sex toys. Some days it amazed her how many toys she sold. Remaining where she was, she placed her hand on the silent alarm button under the display case. "Just let me know if you need help." She made it a point not to crowd her customers unless it was clear they needed assistance and she wanted to keep some distance between herself and the big man in case he tried anything.

"I actually do need help. My friend Elizabeth Porter recommended this place to me," the woman said as she strode farther into the shop, her gold bangles jangling around her wrist noisily.

"Lizzy?"

Smiling widely, the woman nodded. "Yes. We're new friends actually. I just moved to Miami a month ago and my fiancé works for the same company Lizzy and her husband do."

Julieta let her hand drop from hovering over the silent alarm. That explained the man's military-style stance as if he was guarding or casing the place. She tilted her head to the man standing stiffly in the front of her store. "He's with Red Stone too?"

She nodded. "Yes, but he's not my fiancé. That's Ivan Mitchell. He's my personal guard."

Julieta started to raise her eyebrows then caught herself. "Well I'm more than happy to help a friend of Lizzy's. Our mothers go way back and I've known Lizzy since we were kids."

The woman smiled. "That's what she said. She said she's a couple years younger than you and used to follow you around like a puppy dog whenever your parents got together."

At that, Julieta let out a sharp bark of laughter and rounded the counter, all anxiety about the sexy Ivan dissipating. "I don't know about that, but she was quite attentive."

The woman's shoulders relaxed slightly, her sun-kissed arms a nice bronze. "I'm Mina."

"Nice to meet you. You can call me Jules. Why don't you tell me what I can help you with?"

The woman flicked a glance to the front of the store. Julieta followed her line of sight to see the sexy Viking watching them intently again. She squirmed under his glare. It was like he expected her to pull out a weapon at any moment.

Not liking the way he watched her, she turned back to Mina. The tall woman bent slightly, as if wanting to tell her a secret. "I didn't want to bring him but he insisted on coming inside." She let out an annoyed sigh before continuing. "Lizzy said you sold the best lingerie in town and that you sold fun . . . toys," she said in a whisper. Her cheeks tinged crimson and Julieta bit back a smile.

It was always fun to introduce women to their first sex toys. Sadly for her, toys had been her only form of companionship the last three years. Gah, she couldn't even think about that. Nodding, she said, "Are you looking for solo toys or something you can use with your fiancé? Maybe as a surprise for him?" She was just guessing but she'd gotten good at reading her customers the past couple years.

"Definitely with him. And yes, it's a surprise."

"If we can move your scary bodyguard away from the case up front, I think I've got a few things that might interest you. If you decide you like something, I can have it delivered or you can take it with you today—discreetly packaged. And if you don't find anything you like, I have a catalogue you can check out too."

Relief bled into Mina's dark green eyes. "My fiancé, Alex, is coming back tonight from an out of town trip so I'm sure I'll find something."

Julieta nodded and forced herself to ignore the intent stare from the blond-haired, blue-eyed god standing up front as she led Mina to the display case. She'd met enough judgmental men to last a lifetime, thank you very much. Maybe he didn't like the fact that she sold sex toys. Heaven forbid women please themselves on their own. Whatever his problem was, she didn't give a crap. He wasn't her customer and she didn't have time to worry about it.

CHAPTER TWO

Two months later

"You are going to love what I got her," Julieta whispered to Lizzy.

They were sitting next to each other at Mina's bridal shower. Mina Hollingsworth, soon-to-be Mina Blue. The sweet artist was marrying former pro-football player/former Marine Alexander Blue and she was one of the nicest people Julieta had ever met.

"I take it you went off the registry," Lizzy whispered back before taking a sip of her mimosa.

"Just a bit." She held back her grin as Mina picked up her next gift. The black and white damask bag with a bright pink stripe across the top was distinctively from Julieta's store.

"I know who this is from," Mina said, already blushing as she delicately pulled the paper stuffing out the top. Her face split into a wide smile as she pulled out the sheer white, delicate lace lingerie babydoll halter. The back had ruffled layers to create a small bustle and above that in bright pink hand-done stitching were the words 'property of Alex'. Mina's fiancé *might* have mentioned something to Julieta about this.

As Mina pulled it out and saw the back she started laughing, her cheeks flushing an even darker shade of pink. "Did Alex ask you to do this?" she asked.

Julieta just shrugged and pursed her lips together as she fought a smile.

Mina turned it around for the twenty other women to see. Everyone started howling and talking about how much their significant others would want them to get one. Julieta ignored the small pang in her chest. For a bridal shower this one was very small and considering how wealthy Mina was, she was surprised it wasn't bigger. But maybe she shouldn't be. The woman was incredibly picky about who she was friends with—because she wasn't sure who she could trust—and she had guards around her most of the time. All the women at the shower were either married or engaged, except two of Mina's friends from California.

Being single had never bothered Julieta before. The last three years she'd been working like mad to get her business off the ground and now that it had and she was doing well, she had more time on her hands. She had a lot of friends and a huge, loving family but the truth was, she was lonely. When she'd first started her business she'd actually had a serious boyfriend. They'd been together the last two years of college, but once she'd started working long hours he'd decided he couldn't handle it. He'd said he wanted her to be successful and would support her, but in the end it had all been lip service. She was glad she'd found out before they'd taken the next step, but it still stung when she thought about how badly things had ended between them.

She couldn't remember the last date she'd gone on and unfortunately the last two months she'd spent fantasizing about a certain sexy Red Stone Security employee she kept seeing because of her friendship with Mina. But she couldn't get a read on the man. He was always so tight-lipped and gave brooding stares when she was around. She was pretty sure he didn't even like her. Not to mention Mina had mentioned that he was a total player on more than one occasion.

Which made her fantasies even more ridiculous. She wasn't into playboys or bad boys. So why did everything about Ivan make her wake up and take notice?

"Is that from your new line?" Lizzy demanded, shifting against the loveseat in the expansive living room that overlooked the Miami bay as Mina told everyone to go grab food and drinks.

Huge windows and a bright October day made for a gorgeous view and natural lighting as the women broke up and started to eat and mingle.

"Minus the personalized stitching, yes. And *yes*, I've already saved one for you. I can't believe you had a baby five months ago. You look amazing," she said in mock disgust.

"Porter keeps me busy." Lizzy's smile turned mischievous which only made that pang in Julieta's chest expand. ·

She shoved down those feelings as best she could. "Seriously, do you need to remind me how long it's been since I've had sex..." She trailed off as Ivan appeared from out of nowhere.

Wearing his standard dark suit he looked imposing and too sexy for his own good. She gritted her teeth at his timing because she was pretty sure he'd heard her. He so did not need to know she had no sex life. He nodded at both of them politely. For a brief moment she thought he'd approached to speak to her and her heart rate increased by about a thousand percent. That lasted for all of two seconds. The thought of him approaching her just to chat was as ridiculous as her fantasies about him.

"Hey Ivan, where've you been hiding?" Lizzy asked casually.

Since they both worked for Red Stone, though in different capacities, the two were friends. It shouldn't make Julieta jealous that Lizzy, one of her oldest, happily married friends, was so comfortable with Ivan. But it kind of did.

"Mina didn't want us out here for the actual shower but . . . The other two sent me on recon to check out the food. We're getting hungry." He sounded almost sheepish as he spoke, the first time she'd ever seen him look so human.

Lizzy laughed just as Julieta's phone buzzed in her purse. It was laying against her leg and she felt it on her calf. As Ivan and Lizzy started to talk, she snagged her phone and glanced at the incoming text. Even though she'd taken the day off her employees knew they could always reach her for an emergency. As she looked at the screen, all the air fled her lungs in a rush.

You looked fuckable when you left your house this morning. I wanted to shove that cherry dress up over your sweet ass and fuck you from behind. I bet you like it rough whore.

She tried to dismiss the ugly words but bile rose in her throat, swift and nauseating. Abruptly she stood and muttered what she hoped sounded like a believable excuse and hurried across the huge living room area of the luxury condo to the nearest hallway. Her stilettos clicked insistently over the hardwood floors as she hurried to one of the guest bathrooms.

Once inside the bathroom she took a deep breath. The expansive room was all dark wood and frosted glass everywhere. Not that she cared about the décor but it gave her something to focus on other than the revolting text. Whoever had sent it had actually *seen* her, because they'd described the dress she had on. Which meant whoever he was knew where she lived. An unwanted shudder snaked through her.

Today she was wearing a black retro style dress with a sweetheart neckline—with a cherry print. It was the first time she'd worn it too so the person wasn't guessing. Paired with her heels it gave her the pinup look she'd been going for—not something she wanted a psycho to appreciate. She pressed a shaking hand to the middle of her chest and started to drag in a sharp breath when there was a knock on the door.

She opened it and was surprised to see Ivan standing there. "Are you okay?" he asked quietly.

His concern threw her for a loop, but she nodded. "Yeah, great." Her voice sounded all high-pitched and uneven, even to her own ears. She cleared her throat. "Why?"

His eyebrows drew together as he stepped forward, making her take a step back inside. His broad frame took up way too much personal space for her comfort. "You looked shaken."

On instinct her gaze flicked to her cell phone she'd laid on the frosted glass countertop. She met his piercing blue gaze again and shook her head. "I'm fine. Just needed a breather." Seriously, she could hear the lie in her voice and knew he could too. But whatever, there was no way she was telling him anything. She didn't want him to think her life was full of drama and besides, she didn't want a stranger in her business. She could handle this situation. As soon as possible she planned to ask Lizzy and her husband Porter to help her. They were both security experts and had resources she didn't and Julieta knew Lizzy would help with anything. They'd been friends forever.

Moving with a speed and grace she hadn't expected for such a big man, Ivan crossed the distance between them and snagged her phone.

She let out a yelp of indignation but the man was fast, swiping in her code—how had he even known it!—and clearly reading her text. "What are you doing?" she demanded, trying to grab her phone from him, but he just turned to the side, using his body to block her as he read the message.

His savage curse made her freeze as he turned back to her, holding out her phone. "Who sent that to you?"

She snatched it from him with a trembling hand. "I don't know. How did you know my security code?" Julieta couldn't keep the suspicion out of her voice as she took a step back. It wasn't like she truly thought he was the freak who'd been sending her texts the last couple days, but it made her uneasy.

He shrugged unapologetically. "I saw you swipe it in out there."

Okay, his observation skills weren't exactly surprising. The man didn't seem to miss anything. "Well don't do that again. It's an invasion of privacy." She clutched her phone tightly in her fist and crossed her arms over her chest.

When she did, his gaze dipped to her cleavage for the barest instant before his eyes returned to her face. As if he didn't want to look, but couldn't help himself. "You don't know who sent you that?"

She shook her head as a tremble racked her body. And she had no idea who it could be either.

His frown deepened and he started to lift a hand as if he might comfort her but stopped himself. "Is it the first one?"

Again she shook her head, hating that Ivan of all people was seeing her like this. "No, but I'm handling it. And I don't want to talk about it."

Frowning, he opened his mouth to respond when her phone started buzzing in her hand. She jumped then cursed her reaction. It was the number to her shop which meant it was Ruby calling. "This is work," she said to Ivan. "Do you mind?" She looked pointedly at the door.

When he just crossed his arms over his chest and gave her an almost challenging look, she blinked in surprise before annoyance surged up. She so did not have time for this. Turning away from him, she answered the phone. "Hey, Ruby."

"Hey, boss. Someone on a motorbike just drove by and threw a rock through the window. There's something white wrapped around it with a rubber band. It looks like a note, but—"

"Don't touch it." Julieta's heart plummeted. She knew Ivan was still behind her but she couldn't do anything about his presence. "Have you called the police?"

"Yeah, they're on their way and I wasn't going to touch it. And I've also put up the closed sign. Nothing was damaged and no one was injured, but there's glass everywhere and . . . I didn't know what to do."

The dull throb of a headache started at the base of her skull. She closed her eyes and rubbed the back of her neck. "You did exactly the right thing. I'm on my way. If the police arrive before me tell them I'm coming." After they disconnected she took a deep breath and turned around.

Yep, Ivan was still there. And he looked furious.

"Police? What's going on?" he demanded, as if he had every right in the world to ask.

"Nothing I can't handle. It's just work stuff." And she'd ask Lizzy for help before she asked a virtual stranger. She went to step around him but he moved with her.

Frowning, she looked up at him and glared. Even when she was in heels the man still towered over her. At five feet one inch tall she tended to wear four or five inch heels most of the time, but considering he was a little over six feet in height, her shoes didn't give her much of an advantage. She placed her hands on her hips. "Is there a reason you're still in my way?"

"Julieta, I just want to help." The concern in his voice nearly did her in.

She dropped her arms from their defensive pose. "Ivan, I . . . I need to get to my shop. I can't handle..." *Your concern.* But she didn't say that. "For two months you've either ignored me or glared at me so don't be all concerned about me now," she finally snapped before sidestepping him and hurrying from the bathroom. She hated to leave early, but she had no choice so she went in search of Mina and Lizzy.

Owning her own business meant she had to take care of certain things. She just hoped the vandalism and the weird texts weren't related. Hopefully the vandalism was just a stupid teenage prank. Unfortunately her instinct told her the two things were very related and she had a big mess to deal with.

* * *

Taken completely off guard by her dismissal, something that was rare for Ivan, he stared at the luscious backside of Julieta Mederos as she fled the bathroom. What the hell had she been talking about? Ignored or glared at her?

For the past two months he'd barely been able to keep his eyes off her. Whenever she was around he forgot how to think and sometimes breathe. She was the reason he'd come out to the party today. Not for the damn food. He'd known she'd be there and he'd needed to see her like a fucking addict needed his next fix.

And she'd actually said his name for the first time. *Ivan.* God, he'd be replaying that in his head later. Hearing Ivan on her lips—fuck. He scrubbed a hand over his face. He'd fantasized too many times about what it would be like to hear her say his name but under much different circumstances.

He shouldn't be thinking about that. Not when Julieta was clearly facing a threat. Grabbing his radio, he called the other two guys on Mina's security detail and told them to take over. The high rise condo was locked down tight and the building itself had great security protocols, but with the bridal shower today they'd taken extra precautions. Ever since Mina's father had died and her wealth had increased substantially through her inheritance, Mina's soon-to-be-husband had insisted on an increase in security whenever he went out of town. Which hadn't been often the past couple months.

Mina didn't like it, but she loved Alex and she was smart enough to know there were real dangers out there so she lived with it. Especially after what had happened a few months ago. Plus she spent most of her time painting or sculpting in her studio so she was barely aware of her guards for at least eight hours out of the day anyway.

Once the other two guards answered in the affirmative that everything was under control he headed out of the bathroom. At the end of the hallway he waited, watching as Julieta stood talking to Mina, her expression apologetic.

She looked so petite and almost fragile compared to the tall Mina. He couldn't tear his gaze away from Julieta if he tried. He wasn't sure what the style of dress she had on was called, but it was insanely hot. She was petite and curvy and the way the dress flared showed off her toned calves and sexy high heels. He couldn't count how many times he'd fantasized about her draping her legs over his shoulders with her wearing nothing but those heels. Hell, he could actually imagine her digging those things into his back as he tasted her . . . And, he shut that thought down as his pants started to get uncomfortable.

When Julieta made her way to Lizzy near the chocolate fountain Ivan maneuvered his way through the women and politely interrupted Mina as she spoke to one of her friends from back home.

Mimosa in hand, she raised her eyebrows. As usual, paint stained her fingernails. Red today. "Everything okay?" she asked.

He didn't have time for small talk. "What did Julieta say to you?"

Mina blinked in surprise. "Oh, ah, just that a work issue came up and she has to leave."

He frowned at that. Over the past couple months he'd noticed that Julieta seemed to downplay things and didn't like to talk about herself much. Which was frustrating because he wanted to know everything about her. "I heard her on the phone with one of her employees. Whatever happened at work it's bad enough that the police were called."

Mina gasped but he continued. "If you don't mind, she seemed shaken up so I want to head over there with her." Even if the gorgeous woman didn't want him to go with her, it was happening. "Your place is locked down and—"

"Go. The security here is great and you and Alex worry way more than me anyway. I'll be fine. Just make sure Jules is okay. And make sure you update me, okay?"

He nodded and started to leave when Mina lightly touched his forearm. He didn't like to be touched much, but he made an exception for some people. She was one of them. Pausing, he looked back at her.

"Jules is so sweet and she's my friend. And I don't have many so..." Trailing off, she bit her bottom lip. "I've seen the way you look at her," she finally finished.

It took him a moment to realize what she was trying to say. "I would never hurt her." He'd been watching Julieta enough the past couple months to realize that she had the ability to break his heart. Something he'd never imagined possible. He never made it past one date with women. Julieta was different though. He knew that one date, one time with her, would *never* be enough. On a level he didn't understand, that scared the hell out of him.

She was worth the risk though.

Looking wary, Mina just nodded, as if she wasn't sure she believed him. He didn't bother responding as he turned and zeroed in on Julieta who was still talking to Lizzy. As he approached, he could see her visibly stiffen. She was aware of his presence and didn't like it.

The thought made him frown. Yeah, he didn't like that at all.

Both women turned to look at him, but he kept his focus on Julieta, even if staring at her made him lose his train of thought. "Are you ready?"

She blinked at him in confusion.

"I'm taking you." When she started to protest, he tilted his head in the direction of the display of champagne glasses. "I'm guessing you had at least one drink."

"Oh." Her pretty, full mouth pulled into a frown. She glanced at Lizzy then back at him. "I had one drink more than an hour ago. I didn't even think of that."

If she'd only had one, then an hour was long enough for the effect to be out of her system, but he didn't care. "Then I'll take you. It'll put my mind at ease."

Julieta bit her bottom lip indecisively and he had to bite back a groan as he imagined nibbling on it himself. A protective urge swelled inside him as he watched her. He was going to find out exactly what the asshole texting her was up to and how long it had been going on. He was going to make the fucker regret making Julieta so afraid.

"I caught a ride with Charlotte so if you want I can drop your car off at your place. I know she'll follow me then just take me home from there. It's not like you live far," Lizzy said.

Ivan wanted to hug Lizzy as Julieta started to nod. "Well, if you really don't mind..."

Lizzy shook her head. "I don't. It's a couple extra minutes out of my way. And I'll just leave your keys under the floor mat on the driver's side."

"Thank you for doing this," she said as she pulled her keys from her small purse and handed them to her friend. "And I'm going to call you later about that . . . issue. Okay?"

Lizzy nodded, frowning and Ivan wondered if Julieta had even told her what was going on yet. After saying goodbye, she shot Ivan a wary look, but headed out with him.

Once they stepped out into the tiled area where the private elevators were, he tried to find the right words as he slid his security key across the security pad. "I've never meant to glare at you."

Her head snapped up in surprise. "What?"

"In the bathroom you said I've either ignored or glared at you the past couple months." As the elevator dinged he held out his arm, motioning to let her step inside first. Her heels clicked as she moved and it took all his restraint not to glance down at her incredible legs.

"When you first came into my store with Mina you certainly did glare at me. And you've been doing it ever since." There wasn't exactly hostility in her voice, but definite caution.

He didn't like it. "Yes, when I first met you I probably did. I view everyone as a threat where Mina is concerned, at least initially. It's part of my job. Since then . . . staring at you is a more accurate description." But he'd definitely been aware of her that first day. And he'd fantasized about her later that night.

She turned to look at him again, her dark eyes wide. "Stare?"

"Yes. As in . . . I can't take my fucking eyes off you. And I *never* ignore you." No sane male could ignore this beautiful woman so full of life. It was difficult to even get the words out. "Sometimes it's all I can do to not look at you." His voice was guttural and he had no doubt the lust he'd been hiding the past couple months was visible in his eyes now.

She shook her head, her confusion clear. "But you don't like me."

Ivan snorted and forced himself to face forward and stare at the custom-made interior wood paneled elevator doors. "That's not true either."

"Oh. *Oh,*" she said again as if she finally understood what he was saying. Instead of continuing, however, she clammed up and stared straight ahead too, her posture stiff.

He resisted the urge to scrub a hand over his face. Hell, maybe he shouldn't have said anything at all.

CHAPTER THREE

Standing across the street from Julieta's store, he watched as one of her employees swept up the few shards of glass outside. Most had fallen inside, hopefully ruining some of Julieta's retail. The employee stopped as one of the uniformed policeman approached her. She held the broom loosely in her hand and nodded at something the man said. That woman was a knockout too, just like Julieta was. But in a different way. The blonde was flashier and looked like a whore. Someone like that wasn't worth his time.

Julieta was.

Two police cars were parked in front of the store along with an Explorer he knew was also government issued because of the license plate. He hadn't seen who'd driven it, but he guessed it was the man in the suit talking to the owner of the high end jewelry store next door. He was probably a detective since he wasn't wearing a uniform.

It was easy to blend into the crowd of about twenty onlookers. This street was all commercial shops or restaurants, but it was located in an older, established residential area that saw a lot of foot traffic. All the stores and eateries had good security which was why he'd never try to breach her place during or after hours.

Instead he'd opted to shake her up with a little vandalism. He'd stolen the motorcycle and helmet so neither of them could be traced back to him if the police even bothered to investigate. And he'd already ditched both. After the text he'd sent not too long ago he figured this would really rattle her cage.

Just like she deserved.

It was all her fault that he didn't have a job anymore. And he hadn't been able to find a new one since he'd been fired. Which meant he hadn't been able to cover his rent so he was stuck living with his parents again.

Fucking pathetic.

All thanks to Julieta.

He gritted his teeth as he watched the scene, wondering where the hell she was. He'd followed her after she left her house this morning but had lost her in the downtown area. He'd come by her shop in his own vehicle before he'd stolen the motorcycle so he knew she wasn't working.

He just hoped his little rock throwing ruined whatever her plans had been today. She'd ruined his job so he wanted to cause her as much stress as possible. A flash of colorful movement caught his eye and he turned to see Julieta striding down the sidewalk with a tall, blond man in a suit. She must have parked a block or so over.

His entire body tightened as he watched her move. She was beautiful and successful, the type of woman who never looked twice at him. He resisted the urge to rub his hand over himself. Even in this crowd, he couldn't afford to get caught doing something stupid or for anyone to remember him as a pervert.

But he'd think about her later as he stroked himself off. Just like he always did.

His jaw tightened as he looked at the man walking with her. He looked vaguely familiar but he didn't think Julieta had a boyfriend. He'd been watching her for a couple weeks, learning her schedule, and she hadn't even been on a date.

Which made his plans easier. He wouldn't have to worry about contending with anyone when he broke into her home. Not yet though. He wanted her not just scared, but terrified before he took what he wanted.

She'd fucked him over and now he was going to fuck her before he killed her.

If he hadn't lost his job, his girlfriend never would have broken up with him. She'd called him worthless, pathetic, and so caught up in drugs he couldn't even hold a menial job. Drugs had nothing to do with it. Besides, he only smoked pot. He wasn't some loser addict.

No, it was all that bitch's fault.

"I don't think it was a robbery, just vandalism it looks like," a woman in jogging shorts and a tank top said to a woman wearing the same attire.

What kind of woman wore such skimpy clothes in the fall? She probably liked to show off her body, to taunt men like him. He turned away from the women in disgust.

"Yeah, let's get out of here," her friend said.

As they broke away from the crowd a few other on-lookers did the same, taking away some of his camouflage. That was his cue to leave. He didn't want Julieta to see him, to know he was the one behind the damage to her store.

Not yet.

Moving casually, he headed the same way as the two female joggers even though he'd parked in the exact opposite direction. Just to be safe he would double back and grab his car later. Before he turned down a side street he pulled out the burner phone he'd used to text Julieta earlier and sent off another one.

Don't think that blond friend of yours can protect you from me. You're mine.

Laughing to himself as he hit send, he tossed the phone into the nearest garbage can after the message went through. He'd used it for two previous texts to her and he wasn't going to use any of his burners more than three times. Just to be safe.

When targeting a victim, he always used caution. It was why he hadn't gotten caught.

He was too good and the cops were too fucking stupid. Soon Julieta would be all his until he decided he was tired of her.

* * *

Ivan stilled when Julieta grabbed his forearm, nearly stumbling on the sidewalk. He looked down at her to see her face pale and dark eyes widen. They were one shop down from her store but he stopped completely when she wordlessly held out her cell phone to him, the fear on her face like a dagger against his flesh.

Don't think that blond friend of yours can protect you from me. You're mine.

That raw surge of protectiveness slammed through him again like a gunshot. *Fuck.* He wrapped his arm around her shoulders and blocked her as much as he could from anyone across the street with his body as he directed her to her place. "Let's get you to your store," he murmured, thankful she didn't pull away, but wrapped her arm around his waist instead. He had a ton of questions and planned to look into this situation himself, but for now his main goal was getting her inside, away from whoever was watching her.

Using his sunglasses to cover what he was doing, he scanned the crowd across the street looking for anyone who appeared out of place.

As they walked he slid Julieta's phone into his jacket pocket and pulled out his own. He quickly swiped in the code then turned on the camera function. Pressing record, he started videoing the scene across the street as best he could without being obvious. He knew criminals oftentimes liked to see their handiwork, but that was for more violent acts, like arson. Still . . . that latest text had all his instincts moving into high gear. This guy was here and he would want to see Julieta's fear.

When Ivan got a chance he was sending the video to Lizzy in the hopes she could run it through one of her many facial recognition programs. Or at least know someone who could. He was also sending her the phone numbers the texts had been sent from, and he and Lizzy were going to help Julieta figure out who was harassing her.

As they approached the scene, a man Ivan recognized looked up. Detective Carlito Duarte. Surprise crossed his face as he nodded at Ivan. He turned back to the older man with white hair he was talking to, but Ivan knew he'd be making his way to them soon.

"You know him?" Julieta asked as they waited next to the curb.

He continued to block her body with his. A woman who Ivan guessed must be Ruby was talking to a policeman. She gave Julieta a shaky wave when she saw them.

"Yeah," Ivan said. "He's a detective. You know Grant Caldwell?" Since she knew Porter, Grant's brother, Ivan guessed she must. When she nodded he continued. "That's Carlito Duarte, Grant's former partner."

"Is he . . . do you not trust him?" she whispered, her voice shaky as she looked up at him with surprising trust, letting her arm drop from his waist and putting a couple inches between them.

He didn't like the distance but gave her space. Eyebrows drawn together, he shook his head. "No, he's a good detective. Why?"

"You just . . . you look like you don't like him."

"It has nothing to do with him. It's the fucking situation. I don't like that you've been getting texts like the ones I've read or that your place was vandalized the same day. These two things are related and it's stalker behavior." And he was worried it was going to escalate even more. Situations like this didn't go away on their own.

But . . . the truth was, even if he did like Duarte as a detective, the guy was too damn good looking and he didn't want Julieta noticing. Caveman? Yes. But he couldn't help the way he felt. Ivan was straight but even he could appreciate the GQ thing Duarte had going on. Perfect bronzed skin, gray eyes, and model cheekbones. Yeah, he couldn't even believe he was having these thoughts. But she brought out something primal in him.

Had from the moment he'd seen her in her shop two months ago.

Before she could respond, Julieta's employee with long, blonde hair hurried over. "I'm so sorry about the store. I know you had plans today, but at least there's no real damage, just broken glass." The woman flicked him a questioning glance before looking back at Julieta, as if she was asking who the hell he was.

"You did everything right, Ruby, and I'm just glad you weren't hurt." She motioned to him. "This is Ivan. He's a friend."

Friend? Yeah, he didn't plan to be in that category for long.

Ruby's expression was curious but she nodded at him once then wrapped her arms around herself as she moved closer to Julieta. "This is crazy and so pointless. There's never any crime here. I can't believe some ass-hole did this in the middle of the day either. What if there had been kids around?" Even though she phrased it as a question, it was clear she wasn't looking for an answer.

"The police will figure it out," Julieta murmured, but Ivan could hear the insecurity in her voice.

Duarte took that moment to approach, giving them all a polite smile—and a subtle, but appreciative, look at Julieta. Ivan clenched his jaw. She was beautiful. Of course the other man would notice. Didn't mean he liked it.

Ruby murmured something about cleaning up the glass since she'd already taken pictures for insurance and hurried away.

"Surprised to see you here," Duarte said to Ivan as he held out a hand.

"I'm with Julieta." There was an edge to his voice the detective didn't miss.

He gave Ivan a small, almost imperceptible nod. "Ms. Mederos, I'm sorry about your window, but it could have been a lot worse."

"Thank you," she said softly. "Though I'm surprised they sent out a detective for this."

He shot Ivan a quick look before focusing on her again. "This is a nice area and . . . Grant Caldwell called me. Said his sister-in-law Lizzy asked him if I could come down here because you two are friends."

"Thank you. I hope you didn't go to any trouble, but I appreciate it."

He nodded again. "Your employee told my officer that you've got surveillance inside and outside your shop, correct?"

"Yes."

"That's great. We're going to want a copy of your recordings. There were also a couple witnesses who each got a partial license plate. Combined with the video feed I'm hopeful we can get something useful and wrap this up quickly. Situations like this usually end up being petty vandalism unless you have any former employees who have a beef with you?"

"Well, I've received some strange texts the past couple days…" Biting her bottom lip, Julieta looked at Ivan questioningly and he realized she was asking for help.

Duarte looked at Ivan who pulled out Julieta's cell phone. He swiped in the code he'd memorized and pulled up the text stream from the last number before handing it to the detective.

The other man's eyebrows rose as he looked at it. He scribbled something down in his notepad. "These two came in today?" he asked without looking up.

Julieta nodded, wrapping her arms around herself. "Yes."

The detective frowned and glanced across the street at the thinning crowd.

"I recorded the crowd as soon as she got that last text, which was just as we arrived," Ivan said.

Duarte's head snapped around and he nodded approvingly. "Good. Send it to me."

"I will."

The detective looked back at Julieta. "I'd like to talk to you inside where it's more private. I want to go over a list of any employees you've let go recently, anything else strange that's been happening. Basically anything that might be important."

"Of course. Ruby told me there was a note or something on the rock that broke my window. What did it say?"

"Ah . . . it says the word 'whore' in red marker. With what you've just told me, I don't think this is just vandalism."

Julieta sighed, looking suddenly vulnerable. "Yeah, I don't either."

Ivan's protective instincts flared even brighter as he watched her. Whoever had done this wasn't getting away with it. It took all his control not to pull her into his arms and comfort her, but she needed to tell Duarte everything she knew and Ivan had a couple calls to make. And he wasn't sure if she'd push him away or not. They weren't at that level of friendship or anything else yet. "Why don't you head into your store with Detective Duarte and I'll be inside in a sec?"

She seemed surprised he wasn't coming with her but nodded. "Okay."

As soon as Julieta was safe inside with the detective Ivan pulled out his phone and called the first person he figured could help with the immediate issue.

Vincent picked up on the second ring. "Hey Ranger, what's up?" he asked, the Ranger reference to Ivan's Army days.

Normally they gave each other grief about their former military branches since Vincent had been a SEAL before coming to work for Red Stone Security, but today Ivan couldn't joke around. "Hey, you know Julieta Mederos?"

Vincent had been with the company a lot longer than Ivan. "Yeah, man. Jordan loves her shop. She okay?"

"Not exactly. Someone broke the window at her store today. I'm sure she's got insurance but it needs to be patched up before tonight." Which was only a couple hours away. "Since your family seems to know everyone in the city, I figured you'd know someone who could take care of this last minute."

"My mom's next door neighbor owns a contracting business. I'll see if he can send someone down. If not, I'll do it."

Ivan smiled, not surprised by the offer. He'd do it himself, but he wasn't leaving Julieta for a second. "Thanks, I owe you."

"Yeah you do, and I'll collect." His friend's voice was teasing. "I know the address so I'll text you when I find someone. We'll get this taken care of."

"Thanks. Listen, it's not just a broken window. She's been receiving some stalker-like texts too."

"Shit. Is there anything I can do?"

"Not right now. I've just become aware of the texts and I'm going to help her but I wanted to let you know."

They talked for a few more minutes, and after they disconnected he emailed the video he'd recorded to Lizzy with a brief rundown of what was going on and a promise to call her later tonight. First he wanted to talk more to Julieta. Next he sent the video to Duarte. As he was sliding his cell into his jacket pocket he received a text from Vincent. Relief slid through him when he read that his friend had come through and someone was on the way to temporarily board up the window frame.

As he stepped inside he found Duarte and Julieta wrapping up. Standing next to a rack of sheer black and pink thongs, she glanced over as he strode toward her. Julieta smiled tentatively. He forced his mind not to wander to thoughts of what she'd look like wearing one of those thongs and nothing else.

"We're done here so unless you need me I'm going to speak to Ruby again," Duarte said.

Ivan shook his head. "I'm good."

Once they were alone, he went against that voice in his head telling him to give Julieta space and gently cupped her cheek. "How're you doing?"

She blinked in surprise, but actually leaned into his touch for a moment before she pulled back and he let his hand fall. He didn't want to let go though. No, he wanted to slide his hand through her thick hair and hold her in place as he devoured her mouth with his. "Okay I guess. I just can't believe anyone I know would do this."

"You never said if you've let anyone go recently?"

"I . . . fired someone a couple months ago. Right after I met Mina actually. I wasn't supposed to be working the day you two came in, but because he'd called in sick, again, I had to cover his shift." Her dark eyes filled with doubt. "I still can't imagine him sending me those texts though."

"What's his name?" Ivan demanded.

She opened her mouth then shook her head. "I don't think I should tell you."

His eyebrows raised in surprise. "Why not?"

"Because you look as if you're ready to kill someone."

"I'm not going to touch the guy." *Yet.* He kept that to himself though. "Red Stone has resources the police don't. I just want to help." And keep her safe.

"Okay, but only if you promise not to do anything stupid because I really don't think he's involved. River Aguilar is the last person I fired. Before him I haven't let anyone go since I opened almost three years ago."

"River?"

"Yeah, I know. He told me his mother was a hippie type. Not that he's that much different. He was always late and more often than not I'm pretty sure he was high. He's actually the only man I've ever had work for me, but he applied and seemed eager to work. I hired him because I thought he'd appeal to my female clientele, but he was more trouble than he was worth. I fired him two months ago so why would he start bothering me now?"

Ivan lifted his shoulders casually. "Maybe he hasn't been able to find a job since you let him go and he blames you for his problems. Or maybe he's just fixated on you. Even if he's not the psycho bothering you, it's a starting point."

"I guess." Her gaze trailed to the window and she looked back at him, almost apologetically. "Listen, it was really sweet of you to come with me, but you don't have to stay. I'm going to call one of my brothers and see if I can get this window boarded up and—"

"It's already taken care of. I know you'll likely need to go through your insurance company to get the glass replaced but I've got someone coming to patch it for now. They'll get it done before nightfall."

Her mouth opened a fraction, her eyebrows drawing together slightly as if she didn't know what to say. "Thank you, that's . . . just, thank you."

He nodded, not wanting her thanks. "It's no big deal."

"It's a big deal to me. You just saved me a huge headache. Listen, I feel like we got off on the wrong foot before and I'd really like to take you to dinner tonight as a thank you. My family owns Montez's Grill, a restaurant the next block over so we wouldn't have to go far." Her voice shook and the words came out in a rush, as if she'd been practicing them.

Dinner with Julieta? Hell yeah. "I'd love to. But you're not paying."

She pursed her lips together but that wasn't even up for discussion. He might have no experience with relationships but he wanted to take care of her any way he could.

CHAPTER FOUR

As he cruised by Julieta's house for the sixth time, he made a vow that this would be the last. One more drive-by wouldn't hurt. The street was quiet and she should be back in another hour or so.

The police shouldn't have taken more than a couple hours to question her. But she'd have had to get her shop window fixed or patched. He'd forgotten to factor that in. Damn it. He was just wasting his time right now. He wouldn't get another sighting of her today. His jaw clenched and he tried to bury his rage and lust whenever he thought of her.

She was so fucking hot he couldn't tamp down his lust though. For a while he'd even thought she might like him. She'd always been so friendly to him, smiling openly as if he meant something. Then because of her, he no longer had a job and no way to see her anymore. Not without being obvious.

He wondered if she was just playing hard to get with him. Some women did that. Said one thing, but meant another.

He rubbed a hand over his crotch, but stopped at the sight of Julieta's two-door car coming down the road

toward him. Maybe he'd get to see her after all. Adrenaline slammed through him, making his entire body
tremble.

Keeping his gaze forward, he maintained a slow
speed and tried not to look at her. His windows were
tinted so it didn't matter because she wouldn't see him.
But he didn't like the urge he felt, like he *needed* to see
her. If he didn't keep control of himself, he got sloppy
and forgot things.

At the last second he looked over, but it wasn't her
driving. Disappointment filled his veins, the darkness
inside him spreading through him in a surge of rage.
The woman behind the wheel had dark hair and looked
Hispanic but it definitely wasn't Julieta. Frowning, he
slowed even more and looked in the rearview mirror to
see the woman pull into Julieta's driveway.

The vehicle behind Julieta's car did the same, the
truck pulling up to a stop next to it. He couldn't see the
driver, but a moment later the truck reversed then
turned back in his direction.

He immediately turned down one of the side streets
that would loop back around by her house. The subdivision was in one of the older, established neighborhoods
and had multiple signs proclaiming they had a neighborhood watch. He had a plan if he got stopped by anyone. He'd just say he was lost and looking for the name

of a street similar to hers. It was in the next subdivision over so it was believable.

When he looped back by her house, the car was sitting in the driveway, which wasn't normal for Julieta. She always parked it in her garage. Her friend must have been dropping it off. He wondered why, but didn't care as he parked across the street and hurried over to her driveway.

He was taking a risk, but it was dusk now, and he decided to use the cover. His entire body was shaking with a mix of fear and pure adrenaline as he reached her car. If her friend had left the car for her, she'd have likely left Julieta's keys somewhere. He quickly searched on top of all the wheels and behind them, only pausing to glance around the neighborhood to see if he was being watched.

Huge bushes blocked him from her closest next door neighbor but that didn't mean the ones across the street couldn't see him. When he came up empty, he tried the driver's side door and was surprised when it opened.

His palms were damp as he hurriedly searched her car, checking under the mats, in between the seats and . . . Bingo. He grinned as he pulled up one of the cup holders in the back console and found a set of keys tucked under the holder. It had been slightly higher than the one next to it and if he hadn't been looking so intently, he might have missed it. She had a little frog charm dangling from the set.

There was a hardware store in the small shopping center two miles from here. It wouldn't take him long at all to get a copy of her keys made then return them.

This was a sign that he was supposed to find these keys, he was certain. Now he had easy access to her home and work. He figured he'd tease her a little more before he made his move. It wasn't like he had anything else to do thanks to her. And the anticipation of waiting until he got to fuck her, for her to be completely at his mercy, was the most intense adrenaline rush. Hardly anything compared to it.

* * *

For the tenth time in as many seconds Julieta wondered if she'd made a mistake bringing Ivan to her parents' restaurant. They weren't working tonight and the place was within walking distance of her store, which was the only reason she'd originally suggested it. But now she realized her cousins and maybe even her brothers would be here.

Of course they would get the wrong idea considering she'd never brought a date with her to the restaurant before. Not that this was even a date. Just a thank you.

The truth was, she didn't want to be alone right now and she always felt safe at her family's place.

Strangely, Ivan made her feel safe too. Safe and a whole lot of other things she didn't want to be feeling. For months she'd been living with the impression that he didn't even like her. But after what he'd said in the elevator and the protective way he'd been acting since then it was clear she'd been wrong. She had no clue how to act now that she knew he more than just liked her. That maybe . . . he was attracted to her as much as she was to him.

As they walked down the quiet sidewalk she cleared her throat. "I didn't even think to ask if you had other plans tonight. Don't feel like you need to have dinner with me."

Ivan snorted softly but didn't look at her as he continually scanned the street and sidewalk for danger, his body language clear that he was ready for any potential threat. "There's nowhere else I'd rather be," he said with quiet intensity.

The truth lacing his words stunned her. She didn't know how to respond and was thankful when they reached the front door of her family's restaurant. The place spanned two streets because it was on a corner, with outside table seating normally on both sidewalks. Tonight only one side was open because they were renovating the other. No surprise, the limited outside seating was already packed, likely because of the beautiful October weather. The ten round tables situated under either awnings attached to the side of the building or beneath individual umbrellas, were filled mostly with couples. Soft Latin jazz pumped through hidden speakers on the patio as people talked, laughed and drank. Peacefulness welled up inside her at the sight and just like that, she started to relax. "This is it."

"We should have come here earlier," Ivan murmured and she looked up to find him watching her closely, that same intensity in his gaze she'd heard in his voice seconds ago.

She frowned, feeling almost nervous under his intense blue stare. "Why?"

"I like seeing you smile." Before she could respond, he held the heavy wooden door open for her and motioned for her to enter.

Blinking in surprise at the comment, she strode past him, trying to come to terms with this new reality where Ivan liked her. And not in a platonic way. Because she was very attracted to him too, even if she knew it was stupid. The music was slightly louder inside as was the noise level since there were triple the seats in the interior. A vibrant blend of spices teased her nose. Onions, peppers, and something citrusy were the strongest. It reminded her of her home growing up.

They were immediately greeted with a bright smile by one of her younger cousins, Jaidyn. Her cousin wore the standard black pants and short-sleeved black T-shirt every employee at the restaurant had on. Jaidyn's eyebrows rose as she looked at Ivan then Julieta. She leaned in for a brief kiss on the cheek. "*Hola*, Jules. You brought a date *here*?" she asked bluntly, as she stepped back.

Feeling her face flush and cursing herself again for thinking it was a good idea to bring Ivan here, Julieta started to answer that this wasn't a date, but Ivan beat her to the punch.

Wrapping an arm around Julieta's shoulders he smiled easily, drawing out a blush from Jaidyn. Yeah, Julieta figured he had that effect on most women. He was all boyish charm but with an edge that was hard to ignore. "I'm Ivan. It's a pleasure to meet you," he said, holding out his hand.

Surprised by his subtle possessive hold, Julieta didn't correct him as Jaidyn shook his hand because she really liked the feel of him holding her close. She cleared her throat and glanced around, looking for other family members. Yes, this had been a stupid idea. Maybe she could still get out of it. "If you don't have seating—"

Jaidyn waved one of her perfectly manicured hands in the air. "Don't even finish that sentence. *Tu mama* would skin me alive if I ever turned you away. Come on." She tilted her head in the direction of the main seating area then gave Ivan an appraising look from head to toe before turning on her heel.

Julieta inwardly cringed, knowing that soon her cousin would be on the phone with all their other cousins, giving them a full description of Ivan. "I'm going to apologize in advance for any family members you meet tonight." Especially if her brothers showed up. "I wasn't really thinking and—"

"Julieta," Ivan murmured in that sexy, deep voice of his. "Don't apologize for anything. I like that you brought me here."

When he didn't expand on why, she could only make guesses, but couldn't come up with any good reasons why he'd think that. Besides, he wasn't going to like it once he met her crazy family. She loved them all but they were a lot to take in and this wasn't even a real date. It was just . . . what was it? She didn't even know. Certainly nothing serious because she knew from Mina that Ivan didn't do serious. Which was just as well.

Jaidyn led them to a corner table with a limited amount of privacy. When Ivan held out the chair for her, Jaidyn's mouth fell open. Then Julieta's mouth nearly fell open when he took off his jacket and slid it onto the back of his chair. She'd never seen him in anything but his suit and the long-sleeved, button-down shirt did absolutely *nothing* to hide his muscular physique. The shirt was practically caressing his body, showing off the masculine form she'd been fantasizing about for months.

"Thank you," she murmured. Julieta loved his manners and found herself blushing again. God, what was this? She wasn't some virgin teenager.

Her cousin quickly recovered. "Want me to have your server put in an order of croquettes?"

That sounded almost as amazing as the thought of trailing her fingers and lips over all those muscles Ivan was hiding under his clothes. Since he wasn't on the menu, at least not at the moment, right about now she needed some deep fried comfort food. But she looked at Ivan, not wanting to order for him.

His delicious mouth just curved up a fraction, as if he'd guessed what she was thinking. "Order for us."

She blinked at that. Everything about Ivan was commanding and dominating and yes, intimidating. Not to mention she didn't know any men who asked women to order for them.

Ivan shrugged, his gaze surprisingly intimate as he watched her. As if he had all sorts of delicious things in store for her once they were alone. Which, of course, a ridiculous notion. "You know this place, surprise me."

Something about his deep tone sent shivers down her spine. She looked back at her cousin. "That sounds great. And a glass of wine for me. The usual." Because she definitely needed a glass of *pinot grigio* tonight.

"What do you suggest for me? No alcohol since I'm driving." Ivan pinned her with that intense blue gaze again and for a moment it was as if their surroundings fell away.

She hungrily drank in the sharp, hard planes of his face and his full, kissable lips. Everything about him was so hard and edgy except his lips. When she looked at him, he made her think sexy thoughts of the two of them naked, tangled between sheets. She could just imagine what it would be like to look down between her legs and see that blond head buried there, his tongue teasing her, stroking . . . Blinking, she tore her gaze away and found her cousin watching them curiously. "He'll have an *affogato*," she managed to rasp out, fully aware that her cheeks were flushed.

Grinning, Jaidyn nodded. "Good choice."

Once they were alone Julieta turned back to Ivan. "It's a combination of coffee, espresso and ice cream and it's delicious. I think you'll like it, but if you don't, don't feel obligated to drink it."

For a brief moment his gaze strayed to her mouth and his eyes seemed almost electric before he blinked then looked at her again. "I'm sure I'll love it." There was a sensuous note in his voice and she couldn't help but wonder if he was referring to something other than the drink.

"Thank you again for all you've done today." Having someone else to lean on and just plain help out had been such a huge relief. Her family was always there for her, no matter what, but she tended not to ask for help much because she worried they would think she needed it all the time instead of just when she asked. When she'd first opened her shop they'd been against it because they wanted her working at the restaurant. But she'd been adamant about making her own way.

He grunted a noncommittal sound. "Have you told anyone in your family about what's been going on?"

Well, hell. Didn't he just get right to the point? "Not yet. I plan to, but first I wanted to talk to Lizzy and Porter. The first couple texts . . . I guess I thought maybe it was a fluke or something. After today however . . ." She rolled her shoulders once, trying to shake off the sudden shiver snaking down her spine. "My family is incredibly overprotective, which I'm grateful for. I just want to know exactly what I'm dealing with before I tell them and I figured Lizzy, more than anyone, would know how to help."

"Did you go to the police before today?"

"No. But only because the first couple texts weren't bad enough to warrant it. I'm not stupid. If I'd gone to them with two texts they would have had me fill out a report and that would have been it. No crime has actually been committed."

"Until today." His expression darkened. "Tell me about this River. Not to be sexist, but how did you end up hiring a man to work at your shop?"

She lifted a shoulder. "He applied and I was desperate at the time. I'd just lost two employees who graduated college. They'd been with me for years but after graduating, they both found new jobs in their career of choice and I needed someone fast. River is good looking and charming and he was actually good at his job *when* he showed up. He was just too undependable."

"Any hints of violence or sexual harassment, even subtle?" Ivan's deep voice was soothing, making her feel like she could deal with this situation.

"No. He flirted a little with the customers, but it was harmless and friendly. It helped his sales, but there was nothing flirtatious toward me or Ruby, who's been with me practically since I opened."

"And he didn't have a problem with a female boss? Maybe small signs that he had a problem with authority?"

She shook her head. "Not even a little." Biting her bottom lip, she leaned back when their server, a college-aged man named Gerry approached with their drinks.

He smiled warmly at her and gave a polite nod at Ivan as he withdrew his notepad. "Jaidyn told me you wanted croquettes so I already put the order in. Today the filling is cheese. Are you guys ready or do you want some time?"

Julieta knew what she wanted so she looked at Ivan. "Were you serious about me ordering for you?"

When he nodded, there was that hint of delicious wickedness in his piercing gaze that made it hard to breathe.

Somehow she tore her gaze away from him and looked back at Gerry. "I'll have the *medianoche* and he will have the *carne con papas.*"

"Sounds good. I'll put it in as soon as your appetizer comes out. By the way, if you order coffee after dinner I promise not to spill any on you," he teased as he collected the menus.

She smiled as he left and looked at Ivan, whose heated look hadn't dimmed. If anything, it seemed even brighter. "One of the servers spilled coffee on me a few weeks ago," she said, referencing Gerry's comment. "I ordered you steak and potatoes over rice. It's a little spicy but I figured I couldn't go wrong with that."

"Good choice." He was silent for a beat before continuing. "So you fired this guy months ago?"

She nodded, biting her bottom lip again, something she did when she was nervous. When she saw his gaze stray to her lips she stopped. It made her think of what it would be like to kiss him and right now she didn't need that distraction. Even if he was concerned for her, the man was a player from everything she'd heard. "But that's just it, it was *months* ago, I don't understand why he'd start randomly harassing me now out of the blue. It doesn't make sense."

Ivan was silent for a long moment, tapping his finger on the dark wood table. "It could be any number of things. Maybe losing his job was the starting point for other things going wrong in his life and he needed to blame someone. Who knows, but he's a good starting point. You live alone right?"

"Yes." He would have likely picked that up from her conversations with Mina.

"And . . . you're not seeing anyone? No recent exes who could be behind this?" He asked in a way that made her certain he already knew the answer. He'd been around her and Mina enough that she hadn't mentioned any boyfriends or even casual hookups.

But he hadn't been there when the detective had questioned her about that angle so maybe that was why he was asking now. "No. Not seeing anyone and it's been a while since I've dated, so definitely not an ex." She nearly snorted at the thought.

"How long has it been?"

"Are you asking for the situation or for yourself?" she blurted, taken aback by his abruptness. Even though she didn't want to fidget, she trailed a finger down the stem of her wine glass.

"Myself. I'm curious." He didn't even pause as he answered.

His honesty was refreshing but also intimidating. "Awhile." No way was she telling him that it had been about a year—god, had it really been that long?—since she'd gone on a date. And years since she'd had actual sex. It was embarrassing, even if she did have a good reason for it. With her schedule she just had no freaking time, except for one-night stands. And that wasn't her style. Hell, even if it had been her style, she rarely frequented the places where she could pick up a one-night stand anyway. Because when she went dancing, it was usually with her cousins, brothers and friends. She wasn't about to pick up someone with her brothers hanging around. If she was honest, her last real relationship had burned her harder than she wanted to admit to anyone. She certainly didn't love her ex anymore, but the way things had ended had turned her off to dating and men for a while. "What about you? Are you seeing anyone?"

He shook his head once. "I haven't been out with a woman since the day Mina and I walked into your shop."

His words took her off guard so much that her eyes widened. He couldn't mean because of her, could he? No, not a player like him. "Why not?" Because she didn't think he wanted for female company. All he'd have to do was smile and turn on that charm and women would just fall at his feet.

Ivan rubbed the back of his neck, but he didn't take his gaze off her. "I've been trying to figure out the right way to ask you out."

It didn't matter what he'd said in the elevator, his little confession couldn't have stunned her more if he'd tried. And something about his tone told her he hadn't planned to admit that. She wasn't sure what to make of it. "So is this you asking me out on a date?"

He paused, then nodded. "Yes. Tomorrow night."

"Is that a question?"

Those sexy lips quirked up again. "Please go out with me?"

Despite the vandalism and nasty texts today—and the fact that she probably had a stalker of sorts—the day had ended a lot better than she'd expected. She knew things with a man like Ivan would never be long-term. From what she'd heard he just did casual and while that thought burned in a way she didn't understand, it had been way too long since she'd had any interest in the opposite sex and she wasn't walking away from Ivan. "Yes."

CHAPTER FIVE

Ivan steered down Julieta's street for the second time in the last couple minutes. He'd wanted to do a sweep to make sure everything looked normal but he had no clue since he'd never been here before. He'd even texted Lizzy earlier and asked her to hide Julieta's keys in a better place than under the mat like she'd said at the bridal shower. With everything going on, he didn't want her keys in easy reach for anyone. "How's everything look?"

Julieta fidgeted with the folds of her dress as she looked out the passenger window. "Good, I guess. I don't see any strange cars. This is just too weird," she muttered.

He could hear the stress in her voice and he hated it. He also didn't like that she'd seemed so surprised when he'd asked her out. He knew he was good at covering how he felt but damn, he wished she'd had a clue he was interested in her before today. "Do you have a security system?"

Nodding, she turned to look at him, her dark eyes filled with too many emotions. Primarily worry. She wore her emotions right out in the open. He liked that he could read her so well. "It's pretty basic, but yes. The windows and doors all have contacts."

Some of the tension fled his shoulders. "Good. I'd still like to check out your place if that's all right?" He had to remind himself to phrase it as a question. He was used to taking charge of most situations, especially with his job, but he knew with Julieta that he had to play it right and couldn't go all caveman on her.

Her eyebrows drew together a fraction but she nodded.

"What?" he asked.

"I'm just surprised you asked, that's all." There was a slight note of humor in her voice. "I've seen the way you are with Mina," she added, even though he hadn't responded.

Damn, Julieta was more observant than he'd realized. Something he found incredibly hot. "That's my job. This—you—are different." Even if he did just want to take control of the situation.

"Mina's more than your job," Julieta said softly.

He lifted his shoulders, feeling uncomfortable because it was the truth. He'd worked for Mina's father, Warren Hollingsworth, for years before his death and he'd cared for the man more than he'd ever admitted. When he'd died a few months ago it'd been hard. Was still hard. "Yeah."

"Speaking of, are you sure you can take time away right now?" she asked as he steered into her driveway.

Her sporty two-door car was already in the driveway, but Lizzy had texted both of them letting them know it would be here. She'd also emailed Ivan that she was scanning the faces from the video he'd sent her outside the shop. He wasn't sure what kind of program she used or how long it would take, or even if it was legal, but he knew she'd come through. "Yeah, it's no problem." He'd already called Blue, Mina's fiancé, and let him know he needed a few days off, at least.

As they got out of the vehicle Ivan instinctively surveyed the neighborhood for any potential threats. Waiting for her while she got the keys that Lizzy had left in her car, he tried not to stare at Julieta's ass as she bent over and retrieved them from under the cup holder. Tried and failed.

The woman was compact and curvy and he desperately wanted to lose himself in her. He'd always been with taller, more athletic women. He was big and tended to have bed partners he wasn't worried about getting too rough with. Julieta made him forget any type he'd ever thought he'd had.

She was his type, plain and simple.

Had been from the moment he'd walked into her shop and saw her wearing one of those sexy dresses she favored and high heels that defined those toned legs.

Seeing her bent over like that made him think of bending her over the hood of her little car and taking her slowly from behind as he stroked her clit with his finger. He could fuck her for hours. Days. Something told him that once he'd had her, one time would never be enough.

When she straightened, he half-turned and stared back at the quiet street. He felt like a dick fantasizing about her when she had so much to deal with.

And he wasn't going to fuck this up and do what he always did. He didn't want to just jump into bed with her. Okay, he *did* want to, but he wanted to take things slow with her. Well, slower than normal, and get to know her more.

"Got them," she said, smiling at him as she shut her car door.

He just nodded because he didn't trust his voice and followed her up the walkway to her two-story house. He was surprised by how big it was since she hadn't mentioned roommates.

"You don't have to check it out, but I really appreciate that you are," Julieta said as she slid her key in the lock. Her alarm started beeping as they stepped inside, but she quickly disarmed it and turned to face him with a half-smile. "This place is kinda big for just me. I don't even have furniture in two of the bedrooms so it shouldn't take long."

He glanced to the left at the dimly lit living room. One lamp illuminated it, highlighting her bright, eclectic taste. A pale green loveseat was across from a long leather couch. Different shaped and colored throw pillows were on both. A giant throw rug covered a good portion of the dark hardwood floors. Striped ceiling to floor length curtains that made him think of Arabian nights overlaid the front windows. "This place looks like you," he murmured. Vivid, beautiful, full of life.

"Is that a good thing?" The hesitancy in her voice surprised him.

He looked back at Julieta to find her watching him curiously with those big brown eyes. And she was nibbling on that full, lush bottom lip that made him wonder what it would feel like to have her mouth wrapped around his cock.

Getting hard at *that* thought, he tore his gaze away from her and glanced at the stairs behind her. "Definitely good. Bright and cheerful." He couldn't get out more words than that as he took a step toward the stairs. "Do you mind if I check upstairs?" he asked, needing to move and put a little distance between them. His brain threatened to short circuit when she was around. It was a constant thing and threw him off his game. He was always in control except when she was near. Around her all he could think about was raw fucking or burying his face between her legs. Would she be bare or . . . Damn it. This was not helping the state of his dick.

Belatedly he realized she'd said "no problem" so he headed for the stairs and did a quick, but thorough sweep of her place. When he reached her bedroom he tried to ignore the giant king-sized bed in the room, but it was damn hard. All he could do was imagine her stretched out on the multi-colored comforter in one of those skimpy lingerie pieces from her shop. Something sheer that left nothing to the imagination. He wondered if she used any of the toys she sold. Or brought herself to orgasm while thinking of him . . . His erection grew even harder at the thought so he backtracked from her room and barely managed to get himself under control.

Sweeping her place was easy enough because she hadn't been kidding about two empty bedrooms. After securing the upstairs and downstairs he met her back where she still waited in the foyer, arms wrapped tightly around her middle.

That foreign possessiveness swept up inside him again at the sight of her distress, even as subtle as it was. He wanted to reach out and comfort her but wasn't sure if he should, if it was too soon. They'd only gone out once and tonight hadn't exactly been a date. He'd never been in a relationship with a woman so while he knew what to do in the bedroom, he had no clue how to act now. For the first time in as long as he could remember, he was unsure of himself.

"Everything's clear and if you set your alarm system after I leave, you'll be good."

She visibly relaxed, her hands falling to her side and she gave him one of those soft smiles that took his breath away. "Thank you for doing this. You seriously went above and beyond and I really appreciate it."

He didn't want her gratitude.

Moving slowly, he lifted his hand to cup her cheek, giving her plenty of time to stop him or pull away if she wanted. Her eyes widened but she didn't step back.

Instead she took a small step forward, the action letting loose a fraction of the control he'd been keeping on lockdown.

He was just going to comfort her, really. But when she reached out and placed a hand on his chest, his entire body tightened, pulling taut with the kind of raging hunger he'd never experienced except in her presence. She clenched her fingers against his pec and he shuddered.

"Kiss me," she whispered. Her eyes widened in pure shock the moment she'd uttered the words, as if she couldn't believe she'd said them.

Ivan didn't need more of an invitation than that. He ordered himself to go slow, to be smooth about their first kiss, but all that vanished the second his lips touched hers. She was so damn soft. Something electric arced between them, a tangible thing taking them both by surprise.

Feeling almost possessed, he grasped the wrist of the hand she had on his chest then caught hold of the other. Holding her hands above her head, he backed her up against the door in an unmistakably dominant move as he devoured her mouth with his, stroking, teasing, taking. He wanted to take everything she had to offer and then some. He wanted to imprint his mouth on hers so that she felt him after he'd left tonight, that his taste lingered with her when she laid her head on her pillow later. What he *really* wanted was to take her right up against this door, to claim her.

She let out a moan, maybe in surprise, but her tongue tangled with his hungrily as her body arched into him. Even with heels, she was a lot shorter than him so he bent over her, holding her wrists in place just so he wouldn't touch her anywhere else.

Because he was incredibly tempted. He wanted to grab her hips and hoist her up against the door, pressing himself against her fully so that she'd feel what she did to him. But he was already walking a thin line with her, his control damn near in tatters. He wasn't going to lose it tonight.

Not yet.

She made a soft little mewling sound and nipped his bottom lip playfully, her breathing just as harsh and erratic as his. She tasted sweet, like the after dinner coffee she'd had. It had been one of those specialty drinks with chocolate in it and mixed with her natural taste, it made him crazy.

He wasn't sure how long they stood there making out like teenagers, but the feel of his phone buzzing in his pants' pocket jerked him back to reality. Groaning, he pulled his head back from her and dragged in a ragged breath. He couldn't ever remember being so damn hard. His erection was a heavy club between his legs and there wasn't a damn thing to be done about it.

Julieta watched him with heavy-lidded eyes, her full mouth even more swollen and red, all traces of her lip gloss gone. Even though he didn't want to, he let her wrists go, but placed his hands on either side of her head because he wasn't ready to step back from her just yet. The phone call could be important, hopefully Lizzy getting back to him, but right now, all his focus was on Julieta.

"Dinner. Tomorrow." The only two words he could manage at the moment. He knew they'd already confirmed their date but he wanted to hear her say yes again, needed to know without a doubt that he'd see her soon. He felt almost possessed with the damn need because soon he wanted her under him, on top of him, saying his name as she climaxed around him.

Blinking, as if coming out of a haze, Julieta nodded. "Yes."

As more oxygen returned to his brain, he forced his throat to work again. "Pick you up at seven?"

She nodded again.

He let his hands fall and forced himself to step back even though he wanted to bury his hands in her hair and pull her close to him, to tease his tongue against hers again, to kiss and discover every inch of her tight body. "Make sure you turn your alarm on the second I leave." He'd be watching her house anyway, because he couldn't just leave her unprotected, but that alarm was important.

At the mention of the word alarm, some of the lust in her gaze dimmed, likely as reality set back in. "I will."

"And you'll call if anything doesn't feel right?"

"Yes."

There was a long pause as they both stared at each other, their hunger a palpable pulse of energy and damn it, he wanted to kiss her again. Deep down he knew that it wouldn't take much to get her into bed tonight. Not because he thought she was the type of woman to have one-night stands, but because she wanted him as much as he did her. But he didn't push because he didn't want to do things the way he always had. Julieta was different.

She moved away from the door almost reluctantly, and he grasped the handle with a shaking hand. *Shaking.* That never happened. With his current job and his time with the Rangers, precision was everything. He never lost control. He couldn't afford to if he wanted to stay alive and keep his men alive. Not to mention the people he guarded depended on him to keep a level head in all situations. He'd be shitty at his job if he didn't.

So the actual tremor in his hand took him off guard. It was slight and he didn't think Julieta even noticed but he did.

As soon as she shut the door behind him, he heard the lock slide into place. But he didn't move.

"I want to hear you set the alarm." He thought he heard her laugh, then a few seconds later he heard a beep as the system armed.

"Done," she called out and yes, that was definite humor in her voice.

He was glad that even with the crap she was dealing with, she was comfortable enough to relax around him now. Smiling to himself, he headed back to his SUV after doing a visual sweep of the street and a scan of her backyard. Later he wanted to install security lights for her but figured bringing it up now would be too much like ordering her around. From the short time he'd known her, he figured that might push her buttons the wrong way.

And he was all about infiltrating her defenses subtly, because the most primal part of him knew that things between them were never going to be casual, that once they crossed that line, he wouldn't be able to walk away from her. He wasn't even sure how he knew that, but he'd always trusted his instincts and he wasn't about to start ignoring them now.

Once in the SUV, he didn't bother turning it on as he pulled out his cell phone. Lizzy had called as he'd suspected. He immediately called her back.

She picked up on the second ring. "Hey, Ivan."

"Hey, any news?" He didn't bother with small talk. It was late enough and Lizzy had a family he doubted she wanted to be kept from.

"I scanned that video a couple dozen times and pulled everyone's face from across the street except one. A man. He's wearing sunglasses and a hat and the angles just never worked right because he was leaving the scene. Even if it wasn't intentional, stuff like that messes with my recognition software. I pulled everyone's names and some info on the majority of them, mostly from social media. People share way too much—just saying."

He allowed himself a brief smile. "Anything stand out?"

"I've already sent you the file of what I collected, but no. Most of the people either live in the surrounding neighborhood or work at one of the shops. Not everyone though. I know the cops have info on the phone numbers she was texted from but I'm still trying to find out more about those numbers too. Nothing yet, but I'll let you know what I find out."

Ivan rubbed the back of his neck as some of the tension eased from him. It wasn't much, but it was a start. "Can you look into a guy named River Aguilar? He used to work for Julieta, but she let him go about two months ago."

"Yeah, I remember him."

"Listen . . . I know this isn't official Red Stone business so whatever the cost for your time, bill *me*, okay? Julieta doesn't need to know." He didn't want Julieta dealing with anything extra and if he could take some of the burden from her, he wanted to. It was foreign feeling so protective but at the same time, protecting her felt impossibly right.

"Ivan, Jules is my friend. One of my oldest, best friends. I'm not charging anyone *anything* for this. I already gave Porter, Grant and Harrison a brief rundown of what's going on so they know I'm using company resources and none of them care. Jules is like family to me."

Which meant she'd be family to Porter, Lizzy's husband, and the rest of the Caldwell family by extension.

"I don't care how long it takes, we're going to figure out what's going on and help her," Lizzy continued, her voice heated.

Ivan grinned even though she couldn't see him. He'd only known her a few months, but the woman was loyal, something he could appreciate. "Good. And thank you."

She snorted. "Since we're on the subject of Jules, let me be clear, you hurt her, I'll hurt you."

He jerked against the seat in surprise. "Lizzy—"

"Look, we haven't known each other long and I'm not judging, but I've heard from Mina that you like the ladies. And I've seen the way you look at Jules when you think no one is watching. Jules deserves—"

"Lizzy! I'm not going to hurt Julieta. I *couldn't*. Give me some fucking credit," he muttered.

"Fair enough, but you've been warned." Her voice was light, but he knew she wasn't kidding.

Once they disconnected, Ivan leaned back in his seat but didn't let his guard down. He didn't know if he would stay the entire night, but his sixth sense told him he shouldn't leave her alone tonight. Realistically he knew he couldn't watch her 24/7, but things between them had just changed and he couldn't let anything happen to Julieta. Even if there hadn't been a spark between them, he'd want to protect her.

An hour later he was glad he'd listened to his gut. A motorcycle cruised down the street, stopping three houses down where the male driver parked. But he didn't go inside, instead making his way down the sidewalk straight for Julieta's house. The man walked with purpose. It was almost ten o'clock, way too late for a visitor and she'd said she wasn't seeing anyone.

Ivan watched as the man paused at the corner of her yard and looked at the SUV, but with his tint job, no one could see inside. The guy didn't come over though, just headed to the side of Julieta's house, his helmet tucked under his arm.

Ivan's senses sharpened and he withdrew his SIG. If someone thought they could come after her on his watch, they were about to discover what real pain meant. Moving quietly, he slid from his vehicle. He'd long ago disabled his dome light so it didn't come on.

Instead of shutting the door fully, he pushed it so that it almost closed, but didn't connect to the frame. He didn't want any telltale noises to signal that he'd gotten out.

The relative darkness gave him cover as he hurried across the yard, weapon gripped tight in his hand, but with the street lights and other house lights on in many homes along the street, he couldn't blend into the shadows as well as he'd have preferred.

Once Ivan reached the corner of her two-story stucco house, he peered around it.

The man had set his helmet on the small stone entryway outside Julieta's kitchen door. He was bent over the handle, jiggling it.

Weapon out, Ivan rounded the corner. "Put your hands in the air where I can see them," he demanded.

The man froze for a second before his head snapped up. In the dark Ivan couldn't see his face well, but a small light came on next to the kitchen door, illuminating him perfectly.

A younger man with dark hair and dark eyes stared at him in pure shock. Then his gaze landed on Ivan's weapon and his eyes widened even farther.

"Hands up!" he ordered again.

The man started to lift them and some of Ivan's tension lessened. Until he heard the sound of the door unlocking.

Julieta.

CHAPTER SIX

As the door swung open, the sharpest sense of fear slammed into Ivan's chest. On instinct borne out of the need to protect Julieta, he strode forward, closing the distance between him and the unknown man. From what he could see the guy didn't have a weapon but that didn't mean anything.

And Julieta was about to walk right outside to be faced with her possible stalker. It didn't matter that the guy didn't have any visible weapons, hands could be effective and deadly and there was no way Ivan was letting this guy touch her.

"Julieta, don't open the door!" he shouted as it opened a few inches.

The door stopped moving. "Ivan?"

"There's a man out here I caught trying to break into your—"

"I'm her brother, I wasn't breaking in!"

The door flew open and Julieta's eyes widened as she saw the weapon in Ivan's hand, but she held up a hand and stepped in front of the other man protectively.

Ivan immediately dropped his arm, pointing his weapon down.

"This is my younger brother, Sandro," she said softly.

Ivan holstered his weapon and kept his gaze on her. "I saw a man on a motorcycle park a few houses down then head over here. It looked as if he was trying to break in." He wasn't going to apologize for wanting to protect her. He couldn't even force the words out.

"I have a key and who the hell are you? And why are pulling a fucking gun on me?" her brother demanded, trying to step around Julieta, but she held up an arm to block him.

Ivan ignored him and Julieta did the same. "You stayed here to . . . watch my house didn't you?" Her expression softened even more and he realized she wasn't pissed he'd drawn a weapon on her brother.

He nodded. "Yeah. Needed to know you were safe."

She gave him the sweetest smile, but it froze in a rigid line when her brother stepped up beside her, his body vibrating with tension.

"Safe from what? What the hell is going on?" Sandro's voice raised with each word.

Sighing, Julieta tilted her head toward the open door. "Ivan, you want to come in with us?"

He nodded and waited as she practically shoved her brother inside. The guy looked close in age to Julieta and it was clear the man didn't want to go first, that he wanted to protect his sister, which was commendable. But it was also clear Julieta didn't care as she pushed him forward. Ivan did a visual sweep of the side of her house and next door neighbor's yard and home before following them in. He shut and locked the door then turned to find her brother standing with his hands on his hips next to the stove, all his attention pinned on Ivan.

The man opened his mouth to speak but Julieta held up a hand. Without her heels on, she looked adorable. Wearing skimpy black shorts he thought were called yoga shorts and a formfitting T-shirt with her store's logo on it, she was more beautiful than he'd ever seen her. Because he knew this was what she looked like right before she went to bed. Ivan bit back a groan at the thought that brought to mind. If she was going to bed with him, she wouldn't be wearing anything.

"Ivan, this is Sandro, my youngest brother. He lives three houses down and texted me to let me know he was stopping by after work. You'd already left and I didn't know you were staying or I would have let you know. Sandro, this is Ivan, my . . . friend."

Ivan raised an eyebrow, but nodded politely at the man who still seemed to be fuming.

His lips were pulled into a thin line as he looked at Ivan. "I would say it's nice to meet you, but you just pulled a gun on me. Somebody better explain what the hell is going on."

"Your sister has a stalker." When Julieta cringed, Ivan lifted his shoulders. It was clear she was close to her family and they needed to know. The more people who were aware of the situation, the better.

All her brother's focus instantly turned to her and he started talking to her in rapid fire Spanish until she let out an annoyed sound and cut him off with her hand. Ivan loved when she did that. "English for our guest. And *sit*." She pointed to the nearby kitchen table and gave her brother a hard stare. "If you sit and calm down I'll make you my special hot chocolate."

To Ivan's surprise her brother muttered under his breath but moved to sit at the rectangular table. It was higher off the ground, more like a cocktail table, with high-backed bar style chairs and seated four.

"You too," Julieta said, and Ivan realized she was talking to him.

He blinked, taken off guard by her bossy tone until she gave him a cheeky grin.

"If you sit I'll give you some hot chocolate too," she murmured before turning her back on them and pulling milk out of the dark wood-paneled, likely custom-made refrigerator.

"It's worth it, man," her brother grumbled good-naturedly as Ivan sat across from him. "So, a stalker and this is the first I'm hearing about it?"

"We don't know if it's a stalker." Julieta's voice was strained as she pulled a bag of chocolates from one of the cabinets.

He could hear the lie in her voice and had no doubt her brother could too. Ivan cleared his throat and she shot him a glare over her shoulder.

"Fine, it's definitely a stalker." Next she pulled a pan out but refused to look at her brother or Ivan. It was clear she wanted to keep busy. "I've received some sexually suggestive texts and someone vandalized my store today." Her brother cursed but she continued without missing a beat. "I've talked to the police and Lizzy is helping me out and you know how good she is. It's under control. I was going to tell the family but wanted to do it at once so I didn't have to explain everything ten different times."

"When did you receive the first text?" Sandro asked.

"A couple days ago. And I don't want to talk about what it said or anything else right now. I've told you what's going on and I'm just exhausted thinking about it." The strain in her voice was clear.

Her brother's jaw clenched, but he didn't comment. Instead he looked at Ivan. "So where do you come in to all this?"

"I'm helping out with her problem. I work for Red Stone Security and have a lot of experience with this type of situation." Normally he wouldn't explain himself to anyone, but this was Julieta's brother. "And I'll be Julieta's shadow the next couple days, sleeping in her guest room and making sure she's okay." Because he couldn't go home after this. And camping out in her driveway wasn't a long-term option.

Her brother's eyes widened slightly. "Red Stone?"

Ivan nodded as Julieta dropped a wooden spoon and turned to stare at him.

"That's a good idea," her brother murmured thoughtfully. "Or I could just tell Mama and she'll move in with you." He swiveled to face his sister.

Ivan was under the impression that an unspoken conversation was taking place as the two engaged in a staring contest. Finally Julieta let out an annoyed sigh then turned to Ivan, her expression for once unreadable. "You can sleep in the guest room tonight. Tomorrow we're talking more about this."

They could talk all they wanted, but she needed protection and he was trained and capable of doing it. Simple as that. He hadn't taken a vacation in too many damn years and since being hired by Red Stone Security he had a lot of it piled up from when he'd been a private bodyguard for Warren Hollingsworth.

"How long have you been with Red Stone?" Sandro asked.

Julieta turned back to the stove, muttering something under her breath about annoying men, but Ivan didn't mind. He'd rather her be annoyed at him than something happen to her when he should have been watching her.

"A few months, but I was in private security before that and in the Rangers before that."

Sandro's eyebrows raised and he held out his hand in a friendly gesture. "Thanks for your service."

Surprised yet again, Ivan shook the man's hand.

"Our brother Montez was in the Marines. Years ago. I'm sure he'd like to meet you, even if you were Army." His lips curved as he spoke.

Ivan half-smiled and simply nodded.

Frowning, Sandro turned to where Julieta was breaking up pieces of chocolate and putting them in the pan. "I'm hungry, Jules."

Without turning around, she snorted. "Your legs aren't broken and I'm not Mama."

"It was worth a try," he muttered, sliding off the seat. "Speaking of Mama, got a call from Jaidyn earlier. Said Mama knows you brought a man to the restaurant to-night."

Julieta started muttering in Spanish and while he caught some words, he couldn't translate them all. Her tone made it clear enough she was annoyed. After a few moments she caught herself and started speaking in English again, the camaraderie between her and her brother vivid.

Ivan sat back and watched, taking in their teasing. Growing up it had just been him and his dad. His mom had died in childbirth and his dad had been in the Army.

A lifer until pancreatic cancer killed him. Neither of his parents had had siblings so he didn't have any relatives. Maybe some far flung family somewhere, but he didn't know of any. Watching Julieta and Sandro's interaction warmed something inside him. And reminded him how damn lonely he'd been since his dad died.

An hour later her brother left after being fed, with promises of keeping what he knew to himself for at least one more day. He'd made it clear the only reason he wasn't saying anything was because of Ivan's involvement.

As soon as Julieta closed and locked the door behind her brother, she turned to face Ivan. "You don't actually have to stay the night. I really appreciate that you were watching the house. That's so incredibly sweet, but I know you have a job and I'm sure other things you should be doing. I can't expect you to watch out for me. I have a security system, the police and Lizzy are involved and I know to be more vigilant now. I'm going to talk about everything with Ruby and make sure she's aware of how careful to be at the store. And I'm going to tell my family." The words all came out in a rush, as if she'd been practicing them.

Ivan slid off his seat and slowly stalked toward her. He still couldn't get her taste out of his head or the way she'd felt as he'd held her arms above her head, arching into him as if she couldn't get enough.

Leaning against one of the counters, she crossed her arms over her chest. "What's that look?" she asked almost defensively.

Moving in on her, not giving her a chance to slide away from him, he placed both hands on the counter on either side of her, but didn't touch her. Her scent immediately teased him. She must have showered after he'd left earlier because it was slightly stronger now. Something flowery with a hint of vanilla and something that was all Julieta. Pure and sweet, and it drove him crazy.

Julieta immediately placed her hands on his chest. Maybe to push him away at first, but her fingers tightened against his shirt.

"You need help right now and this is the kind of situation I'm trained to deal with. What kind of asshole would I be if I left this in someone else's hands?" He couldn't live with himself.

"So . . . is this an obligation to you?" There was more than a hint of hurt in her question. She dropped her hands and he immediately missed the feel of her touching him, even if it wasn't skin to skin. Soon though.

His lips pulled into a thin line and despite his promise to himself to not touch her, he cupped the side of her face, gently stroking his thumb over her soft cheek. "Hell no. I like you, Julieta. A lot." Way more than was smart. The beautiful woman had already gotten under his skin and into his head, taking up most of his waking thoughts. "I *want* to help, but I don't feel obligated to."

She let out a sigh and slightly leaned into his touch before straightening. "Okay, thank you then. I'll admit I'll feel a lot safer with you sleeping under the same roof."

He wished it would be in her bed, not the guestroom, but it was too soon for that. His gaze automatically dipped to her mouth and when she licked her lips almost nervously, he groaned.

His cock was hard but he stepped back. "I just need to grab my bag. I always carry a spare bag of basic clothes in my SUV," he rasped out, looking away from her and heading for the door, his pants pulling uncomfortably tight.

No touching, he ordered himself. At least not tonight.

CHAPTER SEVEN

The scent of coffee was strong as Julieta descended the stairs. She'd heard Ivan moving around about an hour ago but coward that she was, had decided to shower and get ready before facing him. The thought of coming down to see him in her skimpy PJs from the night before had just seemed like a bad idea. Especially since the mere thought of him got her all hot and bothered and it was impossible to hide her body's reaction. No, she knew that whatever happened with her and Ivan would be short-term so she didn't want him to know just how much of an effect he had on her.

Now she was wearing a halter-style red and white gingham retro dress. She loved wearing vintage style clothing, especially with her curves. Her clothes and heels were more armor than anything else ever could be, especially against a man that radiated such a raw sex appeal. Carrying her heels and purse, she froze in the doorway of her kitchen.

And nearly swallowed her tongue.

Ivan leaned against the counter, wearing nothing but dark jogging pants and holding a cup of coffee. His blond hair was spiked adorably, as if he hadn't combed it yet. The sculpted muscles of his chest and shoulders stood out as he raised the cup to his mouth, a bright tattoo of intricate artwork wrapping around one shoulder and over one pec.

What she'd imagined he might look like was nothing compared to the reality of the Viking god in her kitchen. Her gaze trained on that ridiculously muscular chest and it was like she'd lost the ability to speak. Or breathe. Or, you know, *think*.

He had a smattering of pale hair on his chest that trailed down to his eight pack. The kind of washboard stomach she'd only seen in ads. But he wasn't bulky or beefed up like those workout junkies. He was more toned and lean, as if he was a runner. Her abdomen tightened with a sharp punch of need as she followed the trail of pale hair to the waistband of his pants.

Just like that, her face flamed because all she wanted to do was tug those pants down and see all of him. Every single delicious inch.

What. The. Hell. This unbridled reaction was so unlike her.

She enjoyed sex, even if it had been a while. But she'd always been a take it or leave it kind of girl. When it was good, it was good, and she savored it. Living without it wasn't a problem because, hello, toys. But looking at this perfect specimen of man, she knew her stupid toys weren't going to cut it anymore.

When Ivan cleared his throat, her gaze snapped up to meet his and her cheeks warmed even more. His lips were quirked up a fraction, as if he was fighting a smile. Because he undoubtedly knew the reaction he had on her.

Probably because any female with a pulse who saw him without a shirt on would have the same reaction. Oh yeah, Mr. Player undoubtedly got this reaction all the damn time. Ugh. That thought doused some of her desire.

"You made coffee?" she asked, setting her shoes by the door and her purse on the counter as she moved toward the full pot. It was kind of a dumb question since it was obvious he had, but her voice was working at least. And she managed to sound normal.

"Yeah. Saw different creamers in the fridge but wasn't sure which you wanted." He was already opening the door, his intense gaze on her as he spoke.

"The cinnamon vanilla one is fine. Thanks for making it." She avoided his gaze as she grabbed the creamer bottle from him. She tried to think of something intelligent, or at least coherent to say, but kept coming up blank. Probably because what she really wanted to ask him was if he would please kiss her again. And she didn't want to stop at kissing. Which was ridiculous since they hadn't even been on a date. Not a real one anyway.

"No problem. I just need to jump in the shower, but I won't take long. Figured I'd head to your store with you and meet the crew installing the new glass window. Did you hear back from your insurance company?" he asked.

She knew he'd planned to shadow her, but she wondered if that meant he'd be with her at work too. That thought was a little disconcerting, but she met his gaze. "Thanks. And yes, I checked my email about an hour ago and the company your friend found is covered so I'm good to use them."

His eyebrows raised a fraction. "That's fast work."

"I use a local company, the same one my parents have been using for decades. My dad is actually friends with the owner so I'm not too surprised. Did you sleep okay?" she asked, changing the subject.

His ice blue eyes seemed to darken, his gaze growing heavy-lidded for a moment. "Good enough. I couldn't stop thinking about the way you tasted."

His words set off a nuclear bomb inside her. Her entire body pulled tight, a rush of heat flooding between her legs as she looked up at him. She'd thought about him all last night too, but she hadn't expected him to admit the same thing. "Me too—the way you tasted, I mean. Not me." Her cheeks flushed as she rambled on so she snapped her mouth shut. Their date tonight couldn't come soon enough.

He opened his mouth to respond when she heard a buzzing sound. Frowning, he pulled his phone out of his pocket. He looked at the screen, swiping it with his thumb as he scrolled through a message. Suddenly his frown faded to be replaced by a smile. Sort of. He looked like a predator who'd gotten prey in his sights. It was startling and sexy.

"Everything okay?" she asked as he slid his phone back into his pocket.

Expression shuttered, he nodded. "Yeah, just Lizzy with an update. Nothing much yet. Let me get ready and we can head out together. But first..." He moved to her kitchen table and reached into a small, brown, paper bag. She'd seen it when she walked in and had been curious about it.

"I had a friend drop this off this morning when you were in the shower." He pulled out a canister of pepper spray. "I wasn't sure if you had any and wanted to make sure you carry this with you from now on. It's the best on the market and you can easily slide your fingers through this strap to place this in your palm. It gives you perfect access for your forefinger." He handed it to her. "Try it."

She did as he said and slid her fingers through the opening. Sure enough it fit perfectly in her palm. She twisted the plastic red safety cover to the side and touched her finger to the button but didn't press down.

"Thank you." Before slipping it off her hand she put the safety back on.

"I just want you safe," he murmured, his voice an octave lower than normal. Taking her by surprise, he leaned down and brushed his lips over her forehead, lingering there for just a moment, as if he wanted to do more, but he didn't.

With a sigh that sounded as if it was filled with regret, he pulled back and strode from the kitchen. She understood how he felt because she was disappointed too. She wanted to ask him what Lizzy had said, and planned to call her friend anyway, but was mesmerized by the sight of Ivan's tight backside and ripped back as he left.

The moment he'd exited the room it was as if she could think and breathe straight again. Oh yeah, she was so screwed where this man was concerned.

* * *

Julieta set the portable phone in the cradle, unable to believe how many calls they'd received at work this morning. It was a Monday, not a typically busy day, but she'd been receiving calls from all the concerned shop owners in the neighborhood in addition to normal customer inquiries. Straightening, she glanced around to find Ruby helping a customer and Ivan talking to one of the men who'd helped install the glass pane.

She'd never seen him so casually dressed, but today he wore jeans and a Polo shirt. He stood with his feet slightly apart and his arms crossed over his broad chest as he nodded at something the other man said. His posture was relaxed enough, but everything about him screamed that he was ready to act if anything dangerous should happen. Like a caged lion, waiting to strike anyone who got in his way.

As if he knew she was watching him, his head turned and that icy gaze immediately landed on her. His lips curved up a fraction and his eyes dipped to check her out with no shame, trailing down her face all the way to her bright red high heels then back up again. Just like that her body erupted in flames, going from zero to a hundred and twenty in mere seconds. Her nipples tightened against her bra cups as if he'd actually stroked her. The way he watched her made her feel sexy like nothing and no one else could.

The bell over the door jingled, drawing her attention away from him. Just like before it was as if the moment she broke eye contact, the rest of her surroundings came back in a rush of sensations and sounds. It should be illegal that he had the ability to distract her to that point.

When her brother Sandro strode through, alarm jumped inside her. It was Monday, he was supposed to be working today. He was part owner in a restaurant with her oldest brother, Montez, Jr. And he never just stopped by to say hi.

Before she'd taken two steps, Ivan had already weaved his way through displays of lingerie and was giving her brother a hand shake of sorts. They did that fist bump/shake thing that her brothers always did before hugging. Of course Ivan and Sandro didn't hug. But their friendliness and Ivan's seeming lack of surprise that Sandro was here made her frown.

"Hey, what's going on?" she asked as she approached them, very aware of the racy display of sheer, leopard print purple bras she was standing next to. And the fact that she owned one and wondered what Ivan would think of her wearing it.

"I've got to run out so Sandro's going to hang here for a while," Ivan said, his expression calm.

As if it shouldn't annoy her that clearly he'd called her brother without mentioning it to her. She glanced at her brother. "How did you guys even contact each other?"

Her brother shrugged. "I gave Ivan my number before I left last night in case anything happened."

Gritting her teeth, she looked at Ivan and tilted her head in the direction of the dressing rooms. "Can I talk to you a sec in private?"

His eyebrows pulled together, but he nodded. The beat of the overhead music was slightly louder near the dressing rooms. Instead of rooms with doors, she'd sectioned off five areas with colorful curtains so patrons wouldn't feel suffocated in a tiny space.

"What's wrong?" Ivan stroked a hand down her bare arm, his expression concerned.

She fought a shiver at the feel of his calloused fingers skating over her skin. "You just called my brother without asking me?"

His eyes widened for a moment, like a deer caught in headlights. "Yeah. And that was . . . obviously not a smart move. I'm sorry Julieta, I wasn't even thinking."

Crap. If he wasn't going to defend himself she couldn't get angry. "It's fine. I just don't want to be kept in the dark. I'm so appreciative of everything you're doing, but this is my life. I need to know what's going on, especially if my family is involved."

His jaw tightened a fraction. "Fair enough. I've got some things to take care of today and I didn't want to leave you alone. I figured asking your brother to help was better than one of my friends, even if they are all trained."

The remaining steam of her annoyance completely faded. "Yeah, I love having Sandro around. I don't see him as much since he started working with my brother, Montez."

"That's the one he owns a restaurant with, right?"

She blinked. "Yes, how'd you know?"

"He told me when we talked this morning."

"I'm surprised he's being so nice to you." The words were out before she could censor herself. "I meant, uh…"

To her surprise, Ivan let out a loud bark of laughter, the action completely relaxing his face, making him look years younger and almost boyish. "I know exactly what you meant. I think he's okay with me because he knows I just want to protect you."

It was still a shock. In the past, anytime she'd brought a man around, her family hadn't warmed up to any of them. Especially after what had happened with her ex. He'd been like family, always around for two years, then nothing. "So what things are you taking care of today?" She wondered if she even had the right to ask. Even though they'd kissed, they certainly weren't in a relationship. But he'd said he wanted to shadow her and was leaving her with her brother. She was curious.

"Ah . . . work related."

Something about his tone was off. She narrowed her gaze. "Is this about something Lizzy told you? You're not doing something illegal are you?" she whispered the last part, even though no one was near the dressing rooms. Julieta hadn't had a chance to contact her friend that morning, but she still planned to. "I can call Lizzy right now and find out what you're doing."

Ivan rubbed a hand over the back of his neck in a way she'd noticed he did when he was agitated or concerned about something. "I'm checking out Aguilar today. Just want to see what his schedule looks like and if I catch him doing something he's not supposed to."

"You're going to be following River around?" Her gut clenched at the thought. If River really was the one stalking her, she didn't want Ivan anywhere near him. It didn't matter that he was clearly trained, she didn't like the thought of him putting himself in danger for her. For all she knew River was harmless and not involved in all this, but worst case scenario, he was her stalker and capable of anything.

"Yeah."

"Ivan, I don't like that—"

"Ms. Mederos, sorry to interrupt, but we're done." The man who Ivan had been talking to earlier came up with a paper in hand, likely her invoice.

"I've got my phone on me," Ivan murmured before hurrying away.

Practically *running*. She gritted her teeth and glared at his backside, delectable as it was, for a moment before turning back to the other man. She had a business to run and a lot of stuff to do today. Ivan was a grown man capable of making his own decisions. While she hated the thought of him following some potential stalker, deep down she knew nothing she said was going to stop him.

Once she wrapped up with the glass guys and helped a couple customers, she looked up from the cash register to find Ruby holding up two very different, but sexy outfits. Not the kind of lingerie you wore under your normal clothes, but more for bedroom play. One was a sexy French maid outfit, and while it wasn't the most original, it was one of her best sellers so clearly people loved it. The other was called 'naughty nurse'. The red and white sheer outfit was all satin and ruffles. It even came with a little headpiece with a red cross on it.

"Which one do you like best?" Ruby asked.

Before she could respond, her brother appeared out of nowhere, like a magnet drawn to Ruby. She was pretty certain he'd had a crush on her for a while.

"I think you could pull off both. If you want to try them on I'd be willing to give you a critique." His voice was light and teasing, his grin that charming smile he too often turned on the ladies.

Ruby just rolled her eyes. "First of all, you'd be more than just willing. And I would ruin you for other women once you saw me." Her brother straightened and blinked in shock. Most women just fell all over themselves when he turned that smile on them, but Ruby would never do that. Her feisty employee continued, one eyebrow arched. "Second, I'm not asking for me, I'm asking which your sister likes best for *her* to wear."

It took about two seconds for Ruby's words to sink in. Even though he was twenty-six and he'd dealt with a sister and female cousins his entire life, his ears turned red. "No. Just *no*. I'm not hearing this." He stepped back and held his hands up to his ears as he moved to the front of the store.

Julieta laughed at his quick retreat then turned to look at her friend. "For me, huh?"

"Uh, yeah. You are so going to be hooking up with tall, blond and delicious soon. And you need to be ready. The costumes might be too much though. Might say you're trying too hard." A slight frown pulling at her lips, Ruby set them on the counter and made a beeline for a purple and black corset Julieta had been eyeing when the new shipment came in last week. "No, I think this and crotchless panties."

She bit back a grin. Just because she sold everything a woman could imagine didn't mean she wore all of her merchandise. "And crotchless doesn't scream I'm eager?"

Ruby snorted. "Girl, you should be eager. That man is mouthwatering. And I say that in a non-jealous way. But I will be hating you a teensy bit the next time I see you and you've got that I-had-sex-with-a-god-glow."

"Didn't that good looking detective ask you out yesterday?"

Ruby grinned in that wicked way of hers and flipped her blonde hair over her shoulder. The woman had a bombshell figure, the type Marilyn Monroe would have envied. "Yes, but he's better looking than me so I said no. I can't date a guy who spends more time in front of the mirror than me. No thank you."

Julieta shook her head, doubting that was why Ruby turned the guy down. For as long as Julieta had known her, the woman rarely dated. It wasn't because men didn't ask either, they did. Often.

Her gaze drifted to the rack of corsets and an image of Ivan's heated expression when he pinned her up against her door last night flooded her mind. "Grab me a small." Because she was definitely buying it. And screw the panties altogether.

She wasn't certain what was going to happen with her and Ivan, but deep down she knew that sleeping with him was a foregone conclusion. She knew herself well enough that this type of physical attraction was incredibly rare and she wasn't walking away from what was developing between them. Even if she knew he was a player and this was going to end up being purely casual, as long as she made it clear to him that she wanted casual too, she'd be fine. Or would at least be able to salvage some of her pride when things between them ended.

CHAPTER EIGHT

"We're good without you," Blue said wryly, his voice coming over Ivan's wireless earpiece as he sat in his SUV.

Ivan rolled his shoulders, trying to ease the building tension as he leaned back against the driver's seat of his vehicle. Alexander Blue was Mina's fiancé and Ivan's new boss. Sort of. Blue had worked for Red Stone Security for a while before being promoted to head up one of their East Coast divisions, which included the company's Hollingsworth account—once Mina moved her family's security division over to them. Ivan had been with Mina's father and Mina kept him on, which meant he now worked for Red Stone and Alex, even though his only client was Mina. "I know, I just—"

"I'm capable of watching out for my own fiancée. We're not leaving the condo since I'm working from home today and there haven't been any threats. Besides, Mina's worried about Jules and she'll have my ass if anything happens to her."

Ivan half-smiled, the tension in his chest easing. He was taking time off no matter what because Julieta needed him, but he was glad this wasn't going to affect his job. "Okay, I just wanted to check in."

"We're good. Take all the time you need and don't worry about checking in anymore. I'll let you know if we have any issues."

Once they disconnected, Ivan took his wireless piece out of his ear and set it next to his phone on the center console before he turned down the last road his GPS directed him to. What he was doing wasn't illegal, as Julieta had been concerned about, but he was going to check out River Aguilar. He wanted to see this guy in person and find out if he had a set schedule. If he was her stalker, Ivan wanted to know everything he could about the guy.

Ivan cruised past the two-story house once, taking in the entire street as he drove. It was a dead end road, off a main street in a middle-class neighborhood. Which meant he wouldn't be able to hang out too long without neighbors getting suspicious. At least it was the middle of the morning on a Monday. Most people would be working.

Choosing a one-story ranch style house two houses down from where Aguilar lived with his mother, he parked on the curb under an oak tree. He cracked a window then shut off the engine. It was October, cool enough to sit in his vehicle without baking.

A two-door red car sat in the driveway. A newer model and according to the file he'd glanced at earlier, not something Aguilar or his mom owned. He jotted down the plate and make and model. The yard itself was immaculate, the grass looking as if it had recently been cut and the flowerbeds were also taken care of.

He wasn't a fan of PI work because it was often boring and took forever to yield results. Julieta might not have time for long investigative work if whoever was stalking her got desperate so Ivan wanted to stay in front of the situation.

And he hated that there were so few leads. This guy had just started harassing her seemingly out of the blue, but there had to be a tipping point. The very first text had felt personal. *I'm going to make you pay for what you did.*

Unfortunately there had been no reference to what she'd supposedly done. It could be something as benign as cutting the guy off while driving. Unlikely, but people on the edge didn't need a sane reason to get angry.

Keeping an eye on the house, he settled against his seat and turned on his mini laptop. He could read on his phone but preferred something bigger. After pulling up his email, he scrolled through Lizzy's latest message with details on Aguilar.

It was all basic, but telling about the guy's personality. He'd moved back in with his mom recently, but it looked as if he'd been living with a woman before that for a couple months. A stripper. All the bills had been in her name, but he'd had his cell phone bill address listed there. Before that it seemed as if he'd lived with a dozen different women over the past two years.

No arrests, no violent history, not even sealed juvie files. Aguilar just seemed lazy. He found random work, would hold down a job for a couple months, then when he lost that job it appeared as if the women he was living with kicked him out. Some seemed to keep him around for a month or so, but eventually, he moved out. Without talking to the women or him, Ivan didn't know if it was because he found another woman to mooch off or if they just got tired of him. He guessed it was the women who got tired of him. Which could explain his anger toward Julieta.

After reading the email he called Lizzy, who answered on the first ring. "Hey, was just about to call you."

"Good news?" *Please say yes.*

"Not really, but it's information. I managed to track down the license plate on that motorcycle. Grant contacted Duarte about it. Turns out the bike was reported stolen a week ago. Some college kid who seems highly unlikely as Jules's stalker, but I'm sending you the info on the kid anyway."

He pushed back the disappointment that surged through him. "And you weren't able to track the bike using CCTVs?" Because he knew she'd done it before.

"Unfortunately no." She let out a frustrated sigh. "And I still haven't gotten a hit on who purchased those phone numbers. We already know they're burner phones, but this likely means he bought them in cash." Which left them still at square one. She didn't say it, but he guessed she was thinking the same thing he was.

He cleared his throat. "Listen, there's a car in his driveway now that isn't listed in the file you sent me. Would you mind running another license plate?" He wasn't sure how much she could do on company time.

She snorted. "Of course not."

After he'd given it to her and she promised to get back to him when she got a hit, he said, "Thanks for everything you're doing." Having someone like Lizzy in his corner was a huge benefit.

"No problem, I love Jules. Call me if you need anything. I'm at the office today."

After they disconnected he pulled up the file on the guy who'd reported his motorcycle stolen and realized why Lizzy said she didn't think he was involved. The kid had posted live updates on one of his social media sites around the time Julieta had received the most recent text from her stalker. It had listed his location too: Orlando.

Damn it.

Sighing, Ivan turned off his laptop, set it on the passenger seat and waited. Three hours later he finally got some action at Aguilar's house.

A woman with long, black hair wearing jeans that might as well have been painted on and an equally snug, bright red T-shirt strode out hand-in-hand with a shirtless Aguilar. The man smiled at her as he walked her to her car. Aguilar pressed her against the driver's side door, groping and kissing her for a few minutes before she left with a huge smile on her face.

Maybe he had a new girlfriend.

Ten minutes later Ivan straightened in his seat and started the engine when the garage door opened. Aguilar pulled out seconds later behind the wheel of the five-year-old truck registered in his name. According to the records Lizzy had sent, the guy's mother had bought it for him and was currently paying his insurance. Pathetic.

Tailing him was easy since he didn't go far. His final destination was a small, locally owned bar and grill in a shopping center next to a Publix less than five minutes away. It was nearing four, which unfortunately meant the place wouldn't be too crowded. Restaurants tended to be busy during lunch and dinner but tapered off in between. Could be good and bad for Ivan. He wanted Julieta's stalker to know he couldn't harass her anymore, but he didn't want to tip his hand too soon. The last text the asshole had sent had specifically mentioned her blond friend so the guy knew what Ivan looked like.

Ivan waited in the parking lot as Aguilar got out and made his way inside. The man was dressed casually in jeans, a T-shirt and boots. Inside the dim restaurant it took a moment for Ivan's eyes to adjust.

A hostess wearing a black skirt and a long-sleeved, white button-down shirt smiled broadly when she saw him and stepped out from behind the wooden stand. "Hi, welcome to—"

Her eyes widened as she glanced behind him. Ivan turned to find the woman who'd left Aguilar's house not long ago striding inside, her expression tense. Ivan faintly heard the hostess mutter a curse, but then she seemed to regain her composure.

"Are you meeting someone or dining alone? Or would you like to wait in the bar?"

"Bar," Ivan murmured, trailing behind the dark-haired woman as she headed to the bar. It was situated on the left with a huge rectangle-shaped bar in the middle of it with chairs lining it. There were also booths lining three of the walls, with nothing on the back wall but a door that led to what he assumed was the kitchen.

Seconds later he realized why the woman was there. She stormed over to a booth where a college-aged woman with pale blonde hair sat in a booth with Aguilar.

And they were clearly not just friends if his tongue down her throat was any indication.

"You son of a bitch!" red shirt shouted.

Aguilar's head whipped up and his eyes widened as he saw her. He held up his hands in apology. "Listen baby..."

Ivan headed for the bar, taking a seat as his phone buzzed in his pocket. When he saw the text from Julieta, anger jumped inside him. *Just got another text from him.*

She didn't need to specify who the 'him' referred to. *When? What did it say?* He glanced back over at the unfolding scene of drama as a man who was clearly a manager tried to calm everyone down while the few other patrons in the bar area looked on in fascination. Ivan quickly realized both women worked here from the way the conversation was heating up.

Literally just now. Had my phone on the counter. Said something vile, you can read when you get here.

Unless Aguilar could text and make out with some woman at the same time, Ivan doubted he was the guy. Seemed as if he was juggling a lot as it was. Ivan fought the disappointment that slid through him. It would have made things a hell of a lot easier to know the identity of Julieta's stalker. Because Ivan didn't mind breaking any rules to bring the guy down, whoever he was.

On my way. Stay close to your brother.

It's okay, you don't have to come. Just wanted you to know.

He snorted and shoved his phone back in his pocket. There was no way he was staying away now. Unfortunately if Aguilar wasn't the guy, they didn't have much to go on at this point. Julieta's stalker could be anybody.

* * *

He drove by Julieta's store, angry to see that the window was already fixed. That should have taken longer, should have been more of a strain on her.

Next time he'd smash in the windows of her car. And slash all the seats. That would certainly get her attention. Unfortunately she usually parked along the curb in plain sight near her store and at home she parked in her garage. When he destroyed her car he'd need to take his time, not be rushed. He wanted her to know exactly how much time and effort he put into destroying something of hers.

The last few texts he'd sent she hadn't responded to before he'd disposed of the phones. Not that he'd actually expected her to respond, but her silence only infuriated him.

Like he wasn't important enough for her. His hands gripped the steering wheel, his knuckles turning white as he neared her store. Looking over, his breath caught in his throat when he saw her in the window dressing one of the mannequins.

She bent over slightly, trying to adjust something, and her dress rode up a couple inches in the back. Not enough for him to see what he wanted, but it made his cock flare to life.

He snapped his head forward, not wanting to crash. The adrenaline rushing through him was potent, almost overwhelming. Waiting until he was a few blocks away, he pulled into a busy shopping center and parked near the back of one of the rows so that he was four spots away from anyone.

With shaking hands, he pulled out one of his burner phones from the glove box and turned it on. Barely able to contain his excitement, he texted her. *Soon I'm going to shove my cock in your mouth and then your ass. I'm going to fuck you anywhere I want until you're screaming my name.*

As he hit send, a thrill went through him. He just wished he could see the fear in her gaze when she read it. He laid the phone on the passenger seat and rubbed his palm over himself. He wanted to unzip his pants and take care of his erection but didn't want to get caught. It wasn't worth the risk of ending up in the system listed as a pervert.

Looking around, he saw that there was no one around and no video cameras that he could see. His windows were tinted anyway. Maybe it wouldn't hurt just to touch himself once.

He couldn't drive home like this and it wasn't going away. Not now with the image of Julieta's frightened face in his mind. As he started to unzip his pants, his phone dinged with an incoming text.

His breath caught in his throat. She'd responded.

As he turned on the screen he immediately saw it wasn't from her. It was one of those standard texts from the company he'd bought the phone from telling him how many minutes he had left.

The sharpest sense of rage surged through him. He wiped his prints from the phone, then rolled down the window. With a shaking hand, he tossed the phone out. Of course she hadn't responded. She thought she was too good for someone like him. Soon she'd learn that she was disposable, a pathetic whore. He was going to make her beg him for death. Then maybe he'd give it to her. Or maybe he'd keep her around even longer than he had the others.

CHAPTER NINE

Julieta's place was quiet. Too quiet for her to be inside. It was perfect for his needs.

He'd checked the window of her garage and her car wasn't in it. There were a couple lights on inside but he was almost positive she wasn't home. He'd been tempted to ring her doorbell to check, but just in case she was—and she had company—he didn't want to take the chance.

When he took her, it would be when she was by herself. He wasn't leaving anything to chance.

Now he needed to scope out the interior of her house and figure out where the best point of entry would be later. And the best place to hide if he decided to lie in wait for her. For now he planned to strike in the middle of the night, close to two or three when she'd be in a dead sleep. He'd have to find a window to leave unlocked too, as his backup on the off chance she changed her locks. The possibility that she'd do it in the next couple days was slim, but he wanted to cover all his bases.

A dog barked in her next door neighbors' backyard, the sound obnoxious, as he crept along the interior of her privacy fence. He'd parked along the curb a couple doors down from her place thirty minutes ago and done a quick recon. After he'd discovered her car wasn't in the garage or driveway, he'd parked a few blocks over in a park then jogged by her place.

Since it still appeared empty, he'd doubled around to the street behind hers. He was pretty certain the home behind hers was empty too. Floodlights hadn't come on, but he'd been quick, racing through their yard before scaling the fence into Julieta's. The sun had recently set so he had darkness on his side. Most people would have gotten home from work an hour ago so they should be inside, making this a good time for him to infiltrate her home.

At least she didn't seem to have a dog.

Not that he had a problem eliminating one, but it would take too much time and could be too messy, especially if the animal was a bigger breed.

His heart pounded erratically as he made his way across the decent sized backyard. No pool or any clutter, just a couple of older orange trees. When he reached the back of the house, he tested the sliding glass door. Locked. He tried the keys he'd had made, but none fit. Since he hadn't been sure which key went to what, he'd made copies of all three on her key ring.

Gritting his teeth, he crept to the edge of the house and peered around the corner. Her privacy fence blocked the side door he'd seen from his earlier recon. He hadn't wanted to risk making himself any more visible, but he didn't have a choice.

Moving quietly, he slipped on his gloves, then un-latched the fence. He had a mask to pull over his face, but wasn't putting that on yet. There wasn't much of an excuse if he got caught wearing it. A quick glance out told him no one was there and the neighborhood was relatively quiet except for a few barking dogs in the distance. At least the one next door had finally quieted.

The flash of headlights made him freeze. He stayed still as the lights swept over the fence briefly.

Her neighbor was pulling into the driveway. He took a step back into the shadows of Julieta's backyard, easing the fence door shut behind him, but not fully closing it. He needed to know if her neighbor had seen him.

A car door shut. "Yeah, I just got home . . . No, I need to shower and change then I'll meet you. Yes, I'll be quick..." The woman's voice trailed off as she likely headed inside.

Not wasting any more time, he opened the fence and hurried toward the side door. The second key he tried slid easily into the lock. He twisted it to the side and smiled at the sound and feel of it unlocking.

After another glance around, he eased the door open, his palms sweating in his gloves.

An alarm started beeping, making him jerk in surprise. It continued beeping, giving him time to turn it off—if he knew the code. Damn it! She had an alarm system? There were no signs in her yard or stickers on her windows.

He could run now, or take another risk. The alarm company would contact the police who would then dispatch an officer, but that could take some time. Maybe ten minutes at the most, depending upon how close an officer was. He was betting on seven minutes to be safe. It was possible one of her neighbors would come check but if that happened, he'd deal with the problem then.

Taking a chance, he ducked inside and shut the door behind him just as the alarm started blaring. He pulled out his black cloth mask from his back pocket and tugged it on. Moving through the house, he quickly scanned her lower floor before racing up the stairs. Two bedrooms were empty, one looked like a guest room and the other was clearly hers.

His heart pounded out of control, his cock heavy between his legs when he saw her big bed. He wanted to fuck her there, make her scream in pleasure and pain for him right where she normally slept.

The alarm blared, the piercing sound making him edgy as he hurried to one of her dressers. He opened the top drawer and found sports bras and what looked like work-out T-shirts. Not what he wanted. He went to the other dresser and tugged open the top drawer.

Bingo.

All her panties and lingerie. He picked up the top piece, a sheer red scrap of material, and held it up to his nose. It smelled like a floral detergent.

His rage grew, detonating inside him, clawing at him. That wasn't what he wanted. He threw it on the ground.

Moving to her attached bathroom, he quickly scanned the room, looking for dirty clothes. Everything was neat and tidy. He opened a door to what he guessed was a linen closet and felt as if his heart would jump out of his chest when he saw a small wicker laundry hamper tucked under the bottom shelf, sitting next to a scale.

With shaking hands, he yanked it out. Delicate feminine underthings were the only thing in the hamper. He knew women liked to hand wash stuff like this so that must be why it was separate from wherever the rest of her laundry was. He grabbed out a black thong and green sheer bra and shoved them in his pocket.

Sweat covered his forehead and upper lip as he backtracked the way he'd come. How long had he been upstairs? He couldn't remember. The alarm made him anxious, the effect of the noise giving him a pounding headache.

Were the police nearby?

Instead of heading out the side door, he went through the kitchen's other open entryway and into a living room. Blinds covered the sliding glass door.

His hands were trembling out of control as he lifted the security latch and yanked the door open. Cool Florida air rushed over him, making him clammy as he stepped out into her backyard.

He paused, looking around. He couldn't see anyone. Sirens blared nearby, spurring him into action. He sprinted across her backyard and scaled the fence. He yanked off his mask and shoved it into his other pocket.

Taking off his hoodie, he wrapped it around his waist and made his way back through the neighbors' yard to their sidewalk. With his hoodie tied and tennis shoes on, he looked as if he was out for a run. Keeping his pace steady, he started a slow jog, scanning his environment as he did.

Smiling, he half-waved at a woman walking her dog a few houses down. She smiled back and didn't give him a second glance, which told him he must look normal enough.

It didn't matter that his heart was an erratic beat inside him and he could barely contain the urge to pull out Julieta's thong and shove it against his face, he at least looked normal on the outside.

As he came to a four way stop, he jogged in place, keeping up the pretense, as two black and white police cars zoomed by, only slowing briefly at the intersection.

Oh yeah, they were definitely headed to Julieta's place.

Once they passed, he jogged across the street and somehow managed to keep his pace slow and steady instead of full out sprinting like the fear inside him demanded. He'd been smart so far, he wouldn't get caught because he couldn't keep himself under control.

The alarm was a problem, but it just meant he'd have to take her another way. Her workplace had security, but if he could catch her alone during one of her lunch breaks or directly after her work day, he would be able to take her, even if she struggled.

Tonight he'd outline his plan for his next move, but only after he stroked himself off with her thong. It wasn't as good as the real thing, but it had touched Julieta and soon he'd be rubbing it all over himself.

* * *

Julieta glanced at Ivan in surprise as he steered into the parking lot of *La Playa* Grill. "You sure this is where you want to go for our first date?"

Ivan nodded. "Your brother told me this was one of your favorite places."

She bit back a smile. "It is, but . . . did he also tell you that he's part owner with my oldest brother? And that a lot of my family will be here tonight?"

Ivan snapped a quick look at her before pulling into one of the only open spots. "He might have forgot to mention that." His voice was wry.

"We don't have to eat here. Seriously, there are a dozen places we could pick on this strip." While her parents' place was more reminiscent of the type of food you'd find in her grandmother's kitchen, her brothers' restaurant served seafood with a Cuban flare. There was more variety, which was perfect since it was close to the beach. But she wasn't sure how she felt about Ivan meeting more of her family, especially when she knew this thing between them was just casual.

He shut off the engine. "We're eating here. Sandro can't scare me off that easily. Or at all," he murmured before getting out of the SUV. He seemed more relaxed now that they were away from her shop.

Ever since he'd returned to her store, he'd been hyper vigilant and alert, his anger at her latest text a palpable thing. He'd barely relaxed until she'd decided to beg off work early and let Ruby and Sandro close up.

She hadn't wanted to, but with Ivan at her shop, edgy, like a caged lion, she figured food and some space was what they needed. Plus she wasn't letting some psycho dictate her life. She was excited about this date with

Ivan—even if it was at her brothers' restaurant. Wasn't like her parents would be here or anything, and with Sandro at her shop that meant Montez would be even busier in the kitchen.

She had nothing to worry about. Still, her gut twisted at the thought of Ivan meeting more of her relatives. She appreciated all his help, but she didn't want to give her family the wrong idea about their relationship and if she kept bringing Ivan around, they would. She wanted to say something, but wasn't sure how to broach the subject without sounding like a bitch.

Julieta picked up her purse from the floorboard and had just taken off her seatbelt when her door opened. Ivan was all about the manners, something she loved. It had been a long time since she'd been out with someone, much less someone so respectful. Taking his hand, she let him help her out of the vehicle and was surprised when he pressed her up against the side of the SUV, his mouth crushing over hers in a breath stealing kiss.

Grabbing her hips, he hoisted her up higher against the side of the door so that she was more level with him. On instinct, she wrapped her legs around him, not caring what kind of display they were potentially making. She'd never felt like this before, so physically consumed that she wanted, *needed*, to feel Ivan inside her. It was probably better that this thing between them was casual, otherwise she'd turn into a complete sex maniac and never get anything done. *Right.* That was what she'd keep telling herself.

His tongue danced with hers and he let out a groan that sounded almost frustrated. Just like that, her entire body heated up even more, as if her nerve endings had been doused in accelerant and he'd lit a match. She arched against him, sliding her hands up his chest and linking her fingers together around the back of his neck.

He nipped her bottom lip, biting down a little more than just playfully, the action taking her off guard and making her nipples tighten. Why were they going to dinner again? They should be back at her place and naked. Unable to stop herself, she slid her hand up the back of his neck and through his short hair. He'd looked so sexy with his hair rumpled this morning and she wanted to see it that way again.

Suddenly Ivan pulled back, breathing hard as he let her go. She let her legs fall from around his waist and straightened her dress as he moved in front of her, blocking her body with his. They were in between his vehicle and another, with a wall at the back of his SUV since he'd reversed into the spot. She automatically tensed at his rigid stance until she heard voices.

That must have been why he'd stopped, but it was just a man and woman laughing as they walked across the parking lot, talking about how good the food had been.

"I'm sorry, Julieta," he murmured as he turned to her. The sound of the voices were already fading as the couple walked farther away.

"Why?" She smoothed a hand down her dress more to calm her nerves than anything else.

"I shouldn't have done that out here, not with . . . There's no excuse for my losing control like that." His expression was carefully neutral, so unlike the passionate man she'd been kissing moments before.

Her lips quirked up and she trailed her fingers down the middle of his chest. "I'm not complaining."

At that his expression softened a fraction. "I want to keep you safe. I should have waited until our surroundings were more secure."

That protectiveness made her like him even more. She took a deep breath. "Listen, Ivan. Would you mind if we went someplace else tonight?" Her stomach was too in knots to think about eating at her brothers' restaurant, no matter how much she'd tried to mentally convince herself that it would be fine.

The change in subject seemed to take him off guard. "Meeting your family doesn't bother me."

"It's not that. I just . . . Look, this thing between us is clearly intense, *physically*, but I know . . . I know that this is just casual for you. It's not fair for my whole family to meet you when this isn't going to last. I don't want them to think there's more to this than there really is."

She bit her bottom lip, feeling strange just putting the words out there, but she needed to be honest. She knew she was making an assumption, but he also wasn't correcting her.

Which was telling all by itself. He stared at her for a long moment and she thought she saw the briefest hint of hurt in his icy eyes, but it was gone so fast she must have imagined it. His jaw tightened and he nodded once before palming his keys. "We can go somewhere else."

She started to respond when her phone buzzed in her purse. Normally she wouldn't answer her phone while on a date—though she wasn't even sure this was a date anymore—but with everything going on and the fact that she owned her own shop, she was basically on call during working hours.

It wasn't the store number though, it was her security company.

A heavy ball of dread settled in her stomach. They only called for one reason. Since she used the same company for her store and home, she knew something bad had happened.

CHAPTER TEN

I van stood next to Julieta at her kitchen table with his hand on her back as she spoke to Detective Duarte. He could feel the tension humming through her even though it was clear she was trying to remain strong.

"Like I said, I don't see much missing except . . . undergarments." Her voice cracked on the last word, but she continued. "I'll need to check through everything again, but wouldn't my alarm have scared the intruder off before he could have taken much?"

The detective nodded, his expression grim as he flicked a glance at Ivan. "Yeah. It's odd that he came into your house at all once your alarm went off. Ninety-nine percent of the time, alarms scare intruders away. They want easy targets. Are you sure you locked all your doors?"

Julieta jerked at that. "My mother is crazy vigilant about that stuff and raised all of us to check doors and windows every night. And I'm a single woman living in Miami. No matter how good of a neighborhood this is, I didn't leave my freaking sliding glass door wide open or my kitchen door unlocked." Her voice vibrated with rage, a tremble snaking through her body that Ivan felt under his fingertips.

He just wanted to pull her into his arms and comfort her, even if she seemed to think whatever was happening between them was casual. He nearly snorted at the thought. At first he'd been hurt by what she'd said outside the restaurant. It wasn't until they'd left to meet the police at her house that her actual words had registered. *I know that this is just casual for you.* For *you.* Meaning she assumed he just wanted something short-term. He was going to clear that up with her soon, but he wasn't stupid enough to think simple words would change her mind. She'd no doubt formed an opinion of him, probably after talking to Mina, and she wouldn't be wrong. He'd only ever done casual.

Until now. Casual with Julieta wasn't an option. He shoved those thoughts aside and focused on the detective. He had to restrain himself from snapping at the man who he knew was just doing his job.

"I know that ma'am, I just have to cover everything. I'm going to be honest with you, this doesn't feel random. Not with what's been going on with you. After the newest text you just showed me and combined with the fact that your alarm didn't immediately scare off the intruder . . . that's not good. His texts have escalated into dangerous territory quickly."

Julieta just nodded, another tremble racking through her. Ivan wrapped his arm around her shoulders, pulling her tight to him. He was thankful when she leaned into him. "What do you suggest right now, Detective?" Ivan asked. He would be watching out for her and he and Lizzy were working to figure out who was behind everything, but that wasn't a long-term option.

"Get a gun and a dog. A big one," Carlito said to her.

Julieta blinked in surprise. "Excuse me?"

The man nodded. "You've already got an alarm system, which is good. But with the right tools, they can be disabled. Most people won't know how to, but we know little about this guy right now. All we know is that he's clearly dangerous and willing to take risks. It was stupid of him to take your undergarments, but he risked getting caught for it. That behavior makes him a real threat."

Yeah, no kidding. The fact that the guy took her panties signified his sexual fixation, making him very dangerous.

"I have a gun," she murmured. "And I know how to use it. I go to the range with my oldest brother once every two weeks. It's in my safe though."

"Take it out at night. Getting a dog won't hurt either. They're the best alarm system you can ask for."

"She'll be staying with me for a while, but thanks for the advice," Ivan said. Getting a dog was a good suggestion, but they needed to eliminate the problem of her stalker, period. And he needed her safe immediately. Her house was clearly compromised.

Julieta swiveled to look at him, her dark eyes wide. "Ivan, we can't . . . You can't..." She trailed off, looking back at the detective.

The man cleared his throat and stepped back, clearly giving them privacy. "I'm heading upstairs if you need me. We should be out of here soon."

As soon as the detective had cleared the kitchen, Julieta was already shaking her head. "Listen, Ivan, I appreciate—"

"Don't even bother. You're staying with me." He knew he sounded high-handed. He didn't care.

She gritted her teeth and slid off the seat to glare at him. All earlier tension seemed to have fled her tight body. "Damn it, Ivan—"

"Keep saying my name like that," he murmured. "Do you know how many nights I've fantasized about you saying it under very different circumstances?" He leaned closer as he asked the question so that there were only a few inches between them. He wanted her to understand that he wanted more than a one-night thing with her.

Julieta pulled in a sharp breath. "Don't try to distract me."

He leaned back only because he was distracting himself being so damn close to her. That subtle floral and vanilla scent teased him. "I'm not. I'm just being honest. There's no point in arguing when coming with me is the best option. Your family will be the first place anyone with half a brain will look. It will also put your family members in danger. Even if your stalker has my license plate number, the vehicle I've been driving is registered to Red Stone. I've only been home once since I got involved in this situation and I know I wasn't followed. Not to mention the security at my condo is a hell of a lot better than here. Not that yours is bad, but it'll be much harder for anyone to infiltrate my place. On the off-chance someone tries, they'd then have to go through me." His voice was a deadly blade, sharp and biting.

"You . . . are annoying when you're right," she muttered. "I don't know. It seems like a big imposition. Are you sure?"

"Positive." He'd never been surer of anything in his life.

* * *

"I can't believe I never knew you lived in the same building as Mina." Julieta took a sip of the wine Ivan had just poured for her as she looked around his place.

He sat on the same couch as her, but there was enough distance between them that they weren't touching. Something she hoped to change soon. "It's not as big as hers, but I like it. And Miami. Never thought I'd move to the East Coast, but I find I prefer it."

His place was still spacious, with lots of big windows overlooking the bright and colorful Miami nightlife. The living room had minimal decorations and not many personal touches, but what was there, said a lot about him. Above the fireplace were a couple pictures of Ivan with other men in uniform. All Rangers, she guessed. His furniture was sleek and dark leather with a large, square coffee table that looked like solid wood all the way through. There were intricate carvings all around the sides. She doubted it was something she could pick up from Pottery Barn. Everything else, down to the indigo leaf-shaped lamp on the table next to the couch was unique. Like Ivan.

"You're from California right?"

He nodded. "Northern. I was born right outside of Eureka, but we moved around so much I don't really call any place home. I just always assumed I'd settle in California, but…" Half-smiling, he shrugged and took a sip of his beer.

"Your dad was in the Army too?"

He nodded again.

"And? Come on, give me more. You've met one of my brothers and a cousin and I don't know anything about you." The man was a closed book. Despite knowing their relationship would likely be brief, she wanted to know everything about him.

His blue eyes turned speculative, almost calculating. He straightened against the couch, the movement slight, but she was under the impression that she'd just been caught in a hunter's snare. "Okay," he finally said. "For every piece of information I give you, you have to tell me something in return. Something personal."

"Deal." That was easy enough. "Now you tell me something personal about you."

"Okay. The first time I had sex I was seventeen. We were about to move again and I was pissed at my dad so I went out for a weekend of partying with my friends. It wasn't hard to get fake IDs back then. My friends bet me I couldn't pick up a college chick and I just had to prove them wrong." He looked smug as he said it. "Of course the next morning when she found out I was seventeen she freaked out."

Julieta had no problem imagining him as a cocky teenager sure of himself in the world. "That's a good one and I guess it's my turn. So . . . my favorite color is purple."

He lifted an eyebrow. "I just told you about my first time and you tell me your favorite color?"

"Hey, it's a personal fact. You didn't specify just how personal in the rules. And I'm pretty sure the only reason you told me that story is because you want to know about my first time." She grinned behind her wine glass before taking another sip.

"I want to know everything about you, even your favorite color," he murmured, his blue eyes no longer icy, but molten hot as he watched her from across the couch. "From that pathetic admission I'm guessing you bend the rules when playing games so now I know two things about you."

"I like to play dirty." As soon as the words were out of her mouth she realized how it sounded. "I mean…" She trailed off, sure anything she said now would sound just as suggestive.

His answering grin was wicked. "I know exactly what you meant. And it's my turn again." He leaned forward slightly, his beer still held loosely in his hand. "I've been fantasizing about you for the past two months. A lot."

Heat infused her cheeks, but she didn't look away. "That's what's you're going with for your fact?"

He nodded.

His words sent another rush of heat between her legs. She shifted against the couch casually, trying to ease the building ache. It didn't help. "My first time I was eighteen, in college and it was with my first boyfriend—and it was terrible. Thankfully it got better. Personal enough?"

Ivan's gaze dipped to her mouth for a moment. "Better. How did you end up starting your own business selling lingerie and sexy toys?"

"Uh uh, look who's trying to play dirty now. I get a personal fact first. Then I'll tell you." Heat built inside her as she simply watched Ivan. Being with him like this, relaxed and flirting, almost made her forget that she had a stalker lurking out there somewhere.

He was silent a long moment as he watched her, which didn't help with the heat factor. All he had to do was turn those baby blues on her and she wanted to melt into a puddle at his feet. "The first time I got shot I was twenty-two." His long fingers lifted up the side of his shirt, revealing the left side of his abs and ribs. There was a faint white spider web-looking scar.

She'd noticed it and others that morning when he'd been shirtless in her kitchen but she'd never imagined he'd actually been *shot*. Which she probably should have considering he'd been in the Army and was now in personal security. "Ivan, I'm—"

"Don't say you're sorry, but you *can* say my name again." His voice dropped an octave as he said the last part.

Fighting a smile, she refused to say his name again. "Fine, but I *am* sorry you got shot. That's awful. And you said the first time so that indicates that it's happened more than once." For that alone she wanted to give him a big hug. She was a big baby when it came to pain. Stubbing her toe was cause to call an ambulance. Getting shot? Oh yeah, he deserved a hug and more.

"That would be another personal fact. First you tell me how you got into your business of choice."

"Hmm, fine, but we will go back to that. I majored in business in college, and my senior year for one of my classes we had to break into groups and come up with real life scenarios of different businesses along with projected expenses. Stuff like that. One of the suggestions was a lingerie shop but our group ended up not using it. Still, the idea stuck with me. In Miami there are a lot of high end, specifically couture, shops but not everyone can afford that. So I did a lot of research my final year, and something I kept hearing from my friends and the women I polled was that in addition to higher end stuff, I should include sex toys and costume lingerie.

"Not the Halloween kind, but bedroom only. I liked the idea of staying diversified and keeping a small, discreet section of toys, especially since I've been in the shops that sell only sex toys and games. The majority of them are gross. With my shop women can come in under the guise of buying lingerie or whatever, and pick up some toys too. Because the truth is, some women still feel uncomfortable buying toys for themselves."

"They could just use the Internet," he said.

"That's true, which is why the majority of what I sell in the store I also sell online. Like I said, I'm all about being diversified. And the location I found certainly helped. It's in an established area so I'm not just grabbing tourists or the type of people who shop in Bayside. I get a lot of repeat customers but I also get a lot of tourists who want to feel like they're shopping somewhere in 'real' Miami."

He watched her intently, as if he cared about what she was saying. It was a little unnerving. "How'd your family feel about it?"

She shrugged. "This is another personal fact but I'm giving you a freebie. My parents were annoyed with me, not because of what I'm selling, but because they wanted me to work for them. They just assumed I was getting a business degree and would eventually move into the family business. But my brother Leo was already starting to take over more and more at their place and I knew my other two brothers were planning to open their own restaurant and honestly, I wanted something that was just mine."

"That's pretty brave."

She snorted and shook her head. "Not really. My parents gave me the startup capital."

He lifted an eyebrow. "And I bet you paid them back."

"With interest." Because she'd needed to know she could do it all on her own.

He started to respond when a soft chime sounded. "It's the doorbell," he said, his voice tight as he set his beer down and stood.

Julieta immediately tensed, but then realized her stalker wouldn't ring the doorbell. Still... "I thought you said the security downstairs had to buzz anyone up."

"They do. Stay here." He was moving before she could respond.

Seconds later she heard a familiar female voice and smiled. She'd texted Mina and Lizzy earlier, letting them know she'd be staying with Ivan temporarily. It was a little late, but Mina must have decided to come see her. Julieta was glad her friend cared enough, but as she set her wine glass down she fought the disappointment threading through her that she and Ivan had been interrupted.

Because she was pretty sure that they were headed to something physical tonight. Something fun and relaxing that would completely take her mind off the craziness surrounding her life right now. And not just with anyone, but with sexy, adorable Ivan who made her let her guard down even if she knew it likely was stupid.

CHAPTER ELEVEN

Ivan stared out one of the big glass windows of his living room at the city below but he wasn't seeing much. Everything blurred together in a kaleidoscope of colors. It was after midnight and he knew he should just go to sleep.

Mina and Blue had stopped by unexpectedly to check on Julieta, interrupting the flirtatious conversation he'd been enjoying with her. After they'd left Julieta had looked exhausted so she'd left to take a shower in the guest bathroom and now he was certain she was in bed.

Alone, unfortunately.

He scrubbed a hand over his face but froze when he saw her reflection in the glass. He immediately turned.

Wearing a short-sleeved blue and purple polka dot pajama set and her damp hair falling loose around her shoulders, she looked . . . terrified.

Shit. "What is it?" he demanded, crossing the distance from the windows to where she stood by the hallway.

Wordlessly she held out her phone, her fingers trembling. When he looked at the screen he expected another vile text. Instead there was a picture of a skimpy, black thong covered in what he was certain was semen. The message attached to it said, *There's nowhere you can hide from me.*

He let out a savage curse and started to squeeze the phone in his hand. He was tempted to smash it to pieces so she'd never have to see that picture again, but that would accomplish nothing. When he opened his arms, she immediately fell into them, wrapping her arms around him and burying her face against his chest. She wasn't crying, but her body trembled.

"We're going to stop this guy, I swear." He kissed the top of her head as he gently rubbed her back. His stomach was tight, the tension building inside him that things had turned ugly so quickly.

She didn't respond, just squeezed him tighter before she stepped back to look at him. She didn't drop her hands from holding onto him. "It's so . . . disgusting. It finally set in that a total freakshow was in my house, touching my stuff, and now it's like, I don't know, I just feel violated. I know it's just a material thing but it was mine and he..." She let out a shudder, her fingers digging into his sides. "Should we send this to Detective Duarte?"

Ivan's jaw tightened and he struggled to find his voice. He wanted to beat the shit out of this guy. Hell, he wanted to do a lot worse, but he cut off the dark thought. "Yeah, I'll take care of it right now. I'll let him and Lizzy know. I don't want to leave you alone, but would you mind waiting here for a few minutes?"

"Of course not. I'm fine, that picture just freaked me out." Her voice cracked, but she seemed to gather herself together.

"I'm going to forward this to my email, then send it to them. I don't know, but maybe Lizzy can pull something from the picture." He doubted it, but anything was possible. "Do you want me to make you tea or coffee or something?" He didn't even know if he had tea, but he was sure he could dig something up.

Julieta shook her head. "I'm okay, but thanks. For everything, not just this."

He just grunted, not wanting her thanks. After she settled on one of the couches and turned the TV on low, he hurried from the room, texting Lizzy from his phone. *You awake?*

Lizzy: *Yeah, Maddox is starting to teethe so both Porter and I are up. We just got him down though. Everything okay?*

Ivan: *No, that bastard just sent her a picture. I'm sending everything to your email. Can you pinpoint where all the phones have been dumped on a map?*

Lizzy: *I'll be up for a while so send whenever. And yes. I'll let you know what I find.*

Ivan: *Thanks and apologize to Porter for taking up so much of your time.*

Lizzy. *No prob. And don't worry about that.*

In his home office, Ivan saved the picture in a folder in his email account and forwarded the message and picture to Lizzy and Duarte. He didn't think he'd need it for anything, but he wanted to keep it as backup evidence.

Ivan hated feeling helpless. The foreign sensation pumping through him made him feel just that. In the Army he'd always had a clear target. Now that he protected Mina, the targets weren't always clear, but his objective was. Protect her from danger. Period.

It should be just as simple as that with Julieta. But nothing was simple where she was concerned. Someone wasn't after her for monetary gain; a psycho had her in his crosshairs and they had no fucking leads. It was like he was driving blind.

As another thought entered his mind, he texted Lizzy again. *If you ping the location of the last phone used, can you find the closest neighborhoods to where it was dumped?*

Unless of course they got lucky and she pinged it to an actual residential location, not a Dumpster. He wasn't banking on that though. The guy had been too careful so far.

Lizzy: *Yep*

He loved her succinct answer. Smiling, he turned his computer off and headed back to the living room where he found Julieta curled up on his couch with one of the hand-stitched blankets he'd bought in Afghanistan wrapped around her shoulders. He liked seeing her in his place, using his things, even if the circumstances sucked.

Thoughts of her stalker and the threat surrounding her faded into the background as their eyes met. Here under his roof, she was safe with him. And he was going to make sure she stayed that way.

"You doing okay?" he asked, sitting on the arm of the loveseat closest to the couch. He wanted to sit next to her and pull her into his arms, but he couldn't get a read on her.

"Yeah." She stood and let the blanket slide onto the couch behind her. Picking up the remote control she clicked off the TV. Wrapping her arms around herself, she turned to face him. Only a couple feet separated them. The silence in the room was deafening as she met his gaze again and he hated the fear in her eyes. "Did Lizzy have anything good to say?"

"Not yet. I just emailed Duarte but hopefully we'll hear from him tomorrow." Because unfortunately Julieta's case wasn't a top priority. Though after the picture she'd just received it might move up.

"Tomorrow I'm telling my family everything and I'll probably skip out on work too. I don't want to be even more of an imposition, but—"

"I would have been surprised if you'd wanted to go to work." He'd been prepared to convince her otherwise anyway. "And you're not an imposition so just forget that, okay?" It scraped against his senses that she could even think that.

Nodding, she blinked quickly and looked down. He realized she was fighting tears and his gut twisted. He pushed off the arm and going against all his self-preservation instincts, pulled her into his arms again. Her grip around him was tight, as if she was afraid he'd let go. No way in hell.

She fit so damn perfectly too, as if this was exactly where she was supposed to be. The more time he spent with her, the harder he fell. Especially seeing her so upset like this. She was so strong and independent and even though she was holding up well, this was still clearly hard on her and he just wanted to take care of her.

Holding her tight, he rubbed his hand along her spine, the material of her top soft against his palm. He wished there were no barriers between them and they were skin to skin but it was probably for the best they weren't. She was too vulnerable right now and he didn't want to take advantage.

When she slid her hands under the back hem of his shirt and moved her fingers underneath, his entire body pulled taut. "Julieta?" he rasped out.

"Take off your shirt." Her words were whispered but he'd heard her correctly.

He leaned back to look at her and she finally met his gaze, her nervousness clear. Yeah, she was way too vulnerable right now. That didn't mean he couldn't give her pleasure, help her take the edge off. He might be relationship-challenged, but he had no doubt he could do that for her. "I have a better idea," he murmured, reaching between their bodies.

Her pajama top was short sleeved and button-down with a little logo on a small pocket over one of her breasts. He slid the top button free, watching her expression as he did.

Her breath hitched but she didn't make a move to stop him. It was dim in the living room, but with the lights from the city below and a nearly full moon hanging in the sky behind them, he had no problem seeing her cheeks flush.

When he slid the second button free, she shifted a little under his scrutiny, as if she was trying to ease an ache. Oh, he'd be easing it for her very soon. By the time he reached the bottom button the anticipation building inside him was too much. The flash of her bronzed skin wasn't enough. His erection pushed insistently against his pants, the hunger to see her bare making his body taut with anticipation.

Before he could slide the top off, she did it for him, letting her shoulders and arms dip back as the top slipped soundlessly to the ground.

His gaze landed on her pale brown nipples and the sharpest sense of hunger slammed into him. She might be petite but the woman was curvy with full, lush breasts. Without pause he grabbed onto her hips and pulled her close. The need to possess her was damn near overwhelming.

Wordlessly he lifted her up so that she had to wrap her legs around his waist. Just like in the parking lot, he hadn't had to ask. She was as into him as he was into her. At least physically. He planned to show her that he wanted a hell of a lot more than just sex.

Keeping his gaze pinned to hers, he walked them to the glass window that overlooked his patio and pressed her up against it. "The windows are tinted, no one can see in," he growled, needing her to know that he'd never let anyone see her naked. Would never let anyone see what was his. He knew she was feeling vulnerable now and wanted to make sure she was comfortable with this.

She shivered, her back arching, brushing her hard nipples against his chest. Her breathing had turned erratic as she brought her hands to his shoulders, her fingers digging into his skin.

Normally he liked a little dirty talk, but he couldn't even find his voice right now. He wanted to tell her all sorts of things. Instead, he shifted slightly and dipped his head, feeling obsessed with the need to taste her everywhere.

He probably should have kissed her first or teased her but he captured her right nipple with his mouth, sucking on it hard.

She let out a surprised groan and arched into him again, this time practically pushing her breast into his mouth.

He laughed lightly against her and she moaned again, her fingers digging even harder into his shoulders. God, those sounds she let out were nearly enough to make him come right then. He flicked his tongue against the hard tip, amazed by how reactive she was.

With every flick and tease she writhed against him, her head falling back against the glass as he held her in place. His cock pulsed between his legs, heavy and insistent, but right now wasn't about him. He kissed a slow path to her other breast, just as eager to tease her other nipple.

For so long sex had always been strictly about release. He always made sure his partners came first, usually more than once, before he did, but sex was just that, sex. He'd never had anything deeper with his partners because he hadn't wanted to. Getting involved with anyone past fucking hadn't been worth any risk.

When he'd first met Julieta yeah, it had been purely physical. He'd have to be dead not to notice how sexually vibrant she was. But the longer he'd been around her, the more he'd realized she was a woman worth risking anything for. He wanted to be in her life, to be the first person she turned to whenever she had a problem or just wanted to talk.

Now that he finally had her under his roof, even with less than stellar circumstances, he wasn't letting her go.

Loosening his grip on her hips, he lifted his head back and stared down at her for a long moment. Her full breasts rose and fell, both wet from the teasing of his tongue and mouth. Her light brown nipples were rock hard. It was difficult to tear his gaze away from them as he slowly let her down to the floor.

"Are you stopping?" Her voice was a strangled whisper.

He looked up at her as he went down on his knees. Stopping? No way in hell. Her eyebrows drew together in confusion for all of a second until he grasped the edges of her cotton shorts. As he slid them down her legs, she bit her bottom lip and his entire body reacted. He wondered if she understood exactly how hot it got him when she bit her lip like that.

Soon, he wanted those lips wrapped around his hard length. But not yet. Now . . . If he hadn't already been on his knees, he might have fallen to them as his gaze landed on the juncture between her beautiful thighs.

A soft triangle of hair covered her mound and just like that, his mouth watered. "Spread your legs," he demanded, his voice harsh and unsteady. She stepped out of the shorts, leaving them where they were and did just that.

Julieta had never felt so exposed in her life. Or maybe she'd just never wanted anyone as much as she wanted Ivan. Her body trembled with pent up hunger, aching for him to fill her. Seeing him on his knees in front of her was too much.

The man was seriously built like a god, something his plain T-shirt and lounge pants couldn't hide. And the way he was looking at her, as if she was the most beautiful thing he'd ever seen, made her feel more powerful than she'd ever imagined.

He leaned closer to her spread legs and inhaled. Actually inhaled, like he couldn't get enough of her. She might be comfortable with her body but oral sex was so intimate and this was Ivan, a man she'd been fantasizing about for months, kneeling in front of her as if he wanted to devour her.

Something she was more than on board with. This wasn't about wanting to forget everything either, though she did want to get that last text out of her mind. This was just about Ivan. As they'd sat and talked tonight, before company had arrived and after, she realized she'd fallen a lot harder for him than she'd thought possible. And maybe she wasn't as okay with casual as she'd tried to convince herself that she was. She wanted more with him and wasn't afraid to fight for it.

He'd stepped up and protected her when he'd had no reason in the world to other than he was an honorable man. Even his profession was all about protecting people.

"Put your leg over my shoulder." His voice was a soft growl she felt all the way to her core. And his order was one she had no problem following.

As she lifted her leg and slid it over his shoulder, he looked up at her. With him clothed and her naked she could only imagine the display they created and it made her even hotter, heat flooding between her legs in a rush.

"Next time I do this, you're wearing those red fuck-me heels. I want to feel them digging into my back as I taste you." His words barely registered before his mouth was on her.

He moved so fast, the intimate action taking her off guard even though she'd known what he planned to do. She'd just assumed he'd tease her, work up to it. Nope, Ivan went straight for her clit, licking his tongue over the throbbing bud in one long sweep. His hands pressed against her inner thighs, keeping them spread and open.

Crying out, she jerked against the chilly window and he shifted lower, opening her wider to him as he slid his tongue along her wet slit. Her nipples pebbled tighter at the erotic sensation. She clutched his shoulder with one hand and slid her fingers through his hair with the other. When she dug into his skin and slightly tugged his hair he moaned against her and increased the pressure.

Over and over he flicked and teased her, dipping his tongue between her lips before moving back to her clit. She completely lost all semblance of time as he knelt there, learning what she liked by the sounds she made.

Taking her by surprise, he slid a finger against her opening, testing her wetness before letting out what sounded a lot like a triumphant growl. Just like with his teasing mouth, he gave no warning before sliding a finger inside her.

She released a shuddering breath at the welcome intrusion. Her inner walls clenched around him, gripping him tight, not wanting to let go.

He increased his pressure against her clit, his tongue positively magic as he slowly began sliding his thick finger in and out of her. Her foot dug into his back, her body incredibly open to the pleasure he was giving her. The orgasm started to build inside her, her abdomen clenching the closer she raced toward release.

He growled something against her spread lips that sounded a lot like "Come for me". She lost it, her orgasm ripping free in a rush of sensation.

Closing her eyes, her head fell back against the window as it built and built, her entire body tingling with the freefall of her climax. It was as if all her nerve endings lit up at once, the shock to her system almost too much pleasure. Almost.

As her orgasm started to ebb in slow, pleasurable waves, Ivan slowly withdrew his finger. Immediately she wanted to tell him to push back inside her, but she didn't have the energy. It took effort but she forced her eyes open and looked down at him.

Her body was boneless and if it wasn't for the window supporting her she might have collapsed. A small part of her expected him to look smug that he'd wrenched such an intense orgasm from her the first time they'd been intimate together, but the only thing in his blue eyes was heat.

"Thank you," she whispered.

His lips quirked up and he lazily slid a hand up over her thigh and down to her knee where her leg was still slung over his shoulder. He squeezed lightly. "I could keep you like this all night." A soft, hungry promise filled those words as his gaze dipped to her mound again.

She should be sated, but another rush of heat slid through her and she hoped they were just getting started. Slowly, he slid her leg off his shoulder. She wobbled once as her foot touched the ground, but Ivan grasped on to her hips.

His hands were warm and steady. He only dropped them for a moment so he could stand. In that moment, with her naked, she realized just how big he was. She already knew, but their differences seemed somehow over pronounced now, especially since she was basking in her post-orgasm glow and completely bare to him.

On instinct she looked down at his erection, her eyes slightly widening at the sight of the impressive bulge covered by his pants. She reached for him, wanting to stroke him, to taste him, but he caught her wrist with his hand.

Her gaze snapped up to him. "What's wrong?" she whispered, unable to make her voice carry any higher. She didn't want to ruin the atmosphere between them.

He cupped her cheek with his free hand, rubbing a calloused thumb over her skin. "Not a damn thing. But tonight is about you."

"I want it to be about both of us." Because she wanted to make him lose control too. She wanted a deeper physical connection with him.

He was silent for a long moment, watching her, his expression unreadable. She resisted the urge to squirm. Finally he spoke. "Outside your brothers' restaurant, what you said about me only wanting casual . . . you're wrong. I want something real with you, Julieta. I've never had a real relationship before so some of this is guessing for me, but I know enough that just telling you something isn't going to cut it. I want to show you I'm serious."

She inwardly winced at her assumptions. "I shouldn't have said that. And you don't need to prove or show anything to me, especially not like this. I'm not a selfish lover and—"

"It's not that." His fingers squeezed lightly around her wrist. "And I never imagined you would be selfish. It's . . . I *want* tonight to be about you. You've been through a lot and I just want it to be about you."

There was something in his tone, as if he was unsure of himself that made her pause. Because Ivan *never* stumbled over his words. Part of her wanted to push because she was pretty sure if she rubbed a palm over his erection, he'd cave, but . . . If she was honest, it was insanely hot that he wanted tonight to be just about her. Even if she was dying to finally strip all the barriers between them. "Okay. But next time is going to be about you too."

He half-smiled, the way his lips quirked up making him seem almost boyish and her knees weakened again. "Next time?"

Wrapping her arms around his waist, she moved closer and lifted up on her toes. "Oh, yeah." There was definitely going to be a next time. Lots of them, and very soon, if she had anything to say about it.

CHAPTER TWELVE

Where the hell was she? He slammed his hand against his steering wheel then flinched at the blast of the horn. His palm stung from the impact but he welcomed the pain.

It had been four fucking days. Four. Days. Julieta hadn't been into work or to her home. Not that he'd seen and he'd been by her shop enough times to know. She must be with that blond man. The one he'd seen her with last Saturday.

She was probably fucking him. Stupid whore. She belonged to him and no one else. She thought she could disappear on him? He refused to let her hide.

His hands shook as he turned down the street to her shop. It was Friday and she always worked Fridays. Of course she usually worked every damn day. She'd been so predictable, her actions like clockwork. Until now.

It was why he'd been patient to wait, to take his time building up to when he'd finally kidnap her. Now . . . he needed to see her. After that last text he'd sent showing her how much she affected him, he hadn't sent anymore.

He'd been determined to show some control, to prove to himself that he had restraint. Even if she pushed at his. Women always thought they were smarter than him. Just like his stupid mom, always telling his dad what to do, beating the man down until he had no opinion of his own. And now she wanted him to go to therapy. As if he fucking needed it.

He wasn't going to waste time sitting on some couch talking to an overeducated asshole who looked down on him, thought they were better than him. No way in hell. Besides, what he needed was Julieta, screaming for him as he cut her, fucked her, and killed her.

He was definitely going to keep her alive for days now, make her beg for death. She didn't get to hide from him. His heart jumped in his throat as he spotted her car a few parking spots down from the outside of her store. He couldn't stop the erratic thump in his chest as he cruised by her store, sticking to the speed limit.

She was *inside*. Finally.

For a moment, it was as if everything around him faded away as he watched her talking to that blonde slut who worked with her. Julieta smiled as she arranged something in the window. She didn't look afraid, like she'd been up worrying about what text he'd send next or where he'd strike; her house or store.

For days he'd imagined her losing sleep as she fought fear of the unknown. Of him. Of what he'd do next. He'd stroked himself off countless times as he fantasized about her living in terror.

But she was practically glowing, like she didn't have a care in the world. Rage detonated inside him, making his entire body shake.

He forced his gaze straight ahead, his vision going hazy for a moment as the anger inside him bubbled higher and higher.

He knew what he had to do. She was going to find out there was nothing he wouldn't do to have her. It didn't matter that she was behind the glass windows and doors of her store. She wasn't safe, even surrounded by people.

He was going to show her exactly how powerful he was. What kind of man he was.

And then he'd take her life.

* * *

Julieta's gaze turned toward the front of her store as the bell over the door jingled. For a moment she thought they had more customers but it was just the two women who'd been shopping finally leaving. They'd been browsing the past hour and had bought a ton of merchandise, which normally made her happy.

She just wanted today to be over. Which was probably a little ungrateful of her, but she was mentally exhausted. She felt like she was constantly looking over her shoulder and expecting her stalker to jump out of the shadows.

For four days she'd been hibernating at Ivan's but she'd finally had enough this morning. Ivan hadn't wanted her to leave at all; he'd been fine with her cooped up under his roof. If she was honest, when she hadn't been focused on the reason she was hiding out, it had been a lot of fun just hanging out with Ivan. They'd been intimate and she'd slept in his bed every night with him holding her—though he was still keeping her at arm's length as far as sex went. He had way more patience than her. They'd also cooked together, watched movies, and thankfully he was like her and didn't mind the quiet so when she'd wanted to read, he'd read too.

She came from a huge family so having actual quiet time to read or just check her email was a miracle. Because living by herself didn't mean she had privacy. One of her brothers, cousins, parents or aunts was always stopping by. Something she loved. But still, a little privacy would be nice.

Over the past four days she'd gotten to know Ivan a lot more too. He'd been in the Army for eight years before working for Mina's father and it was clear that Ivan had really cared for the man. He'd lost his own mother during childbirth then his father to cancer. Now he was basically alone. Well, not alone. He had a lot of friends from the Army and in his current job, but she'd heard the longing in his voice more than once when he told her how lucky she was to have such a supportive family. And she was, of that she had no doubt.

Now that she'd come to her store she was starting to feel somewhat normal again. Not safe exactly, because she wasn't stupid. Just because her stalker had been quiet the past few days didn't mean anything. There were any number of reasons he could have stopped bothering her, but she knew he hadn't just forgotten about her. No, he was still out there. Somewhere. Damn it, if she just knew what he looked like, it would ease some of her tension.

Everywhere she looked she wondered if her stalker was nearby, watching, waiting. As she hung up a silky, purple robe someone had left in the dressing room, she mentally shook herself.

"You look deep in thought," Ivan said, his voice making her jump a little.

She turned from the rack she'd just hung the robe on and smiled at him. He'd been with her all day as she'd made the rounds to her family's restaurants and then her shop. She'd been determined to get out and stop living in fear. It amazed her that she wasn't sick of Ivan *and* that he wasn't tired of her. If anything, she wanted to spend more time with him. "Just thinking of you and . . . later tonight." Because after four days of sharing the same bed with him and no sex, and she was about to

crawl out of her skin. She needed a deeper physical connection. She felt like she'd been waiting for Ivan for
years.

"Do not rub it in that you're getting some and I'm
alone," Ruby said as she emerged from the storeroom,
carrying a dozen of the 'sexy policewoman' costumes
that had arrived today.

Ivan didn't say anything, but his lips quirked up as he
gave Julieta a quick kiss on the mouth before retreating
to her office. The store's security setup was in there,
with cameras showing the outside and inside of the store
at various angles. She knew he was uber-concerned with
keeping an eye on everything today—and so was she—
but she also figured that he wasn't used to Ruby's brand
of, well, everything.

Ruby grinned. "Didn't mean to scare him off."

"Liar. You like scaring men." Julieta rolled her eyes as
she headed for one of the display cases. She'd tucked a
file Ivan had given her on the shelf under the cash register. Since it was quiet and almost closing time, she wanted to look at it one more time. Even if she knew it
would just frustrate her.

"Anything special you want me to do before closing?"
Ruby asked as she made room for the new arrivals.

"Not today. Just make sure the display case at the
front is wiped down and run the end of day reports. I
think I'll close up in fifteen minutes if no one else comes

in." Normally she ran the reports, but this past week Ruby had really stepped up and Julieta realized she needed to start delegating more duties if she ever wanted to take a real vacation or just have a life. She loved her job but it was incredibly nice to be able to depend on someone else.

She opened the file on the glass top and started scanning the names and addresses from the neighborhoods surrounding where that freak had dumped the last phone he'd used to text her. It was probably pointless since she'd read over the thing dozens of times and didn't recognize any of the names, but she wanted to be doing something. As she started scanning it, her cell buzzed in the nearly seamless pocket of her fifties style black and red dress that flared out from her waist. She'd worn it today because Ivan liked her cherry red heels and they matched the dress.

Her fingers grazed the pepper spray she'd tucked in there as she pulled her phone out. Without looking at the screen she knew it was her mom because of the ringtone.

"Hey, Mama."

"*Mi linda*, how are you feeling? Everything okay?"

She smiled at her mom's concern, grateful she had such a good mother. "I'm good, I promise. Ivan is here with me and we'll probably be closing up shop soon anyway."

"Why don't you two and Ruby come down to the restaurant after you close? I've already got a table saved for you." Oh yeah, her mama wasn't asking.

If she'd saved a table, this was more or less a demand. "Ivan and I will be there but I'm not sure about Ruby."

Her mom made a soft tsking sound. "Tell Ruby that Montez will be here. He's stopping by too. She'll come."

Montez? "Do you mean Sandro?"

"No, I know the difference between my sons. You just tell her and see if she doesn't come." Her mom had that knowing tone of voice that made Julieta's eyebrows shoot up.

Her oldest brother had been scarred badly in Afghanistan and as far as Julieta knew he didn't date anymore. And she also didn't think Ruby had ever met her oldest brother. Her mom must be confused. But she knew better than to argue with her. "Okay, I'll tell her."

"Good. Listen, this is probably me being a paranoid mother, but I got a call from the unemployment department today. They contact employers regarding former employees who file for . . . Well, that's not important. The call made me think of something. Do you remember Buck Howell?"

"No." But the name sounded vaguely familiar. She glanced down at the file in front of her, moving out of the way as Ruby stepped up behind her to start running the reports.

"Well, he's a server we had who was incredibly inept. He's the one who spilled that hot coffee all over you."

"Oh right, the creepy one." She'd never known his name, he hadn't even been at her parents' restaurant long.

"It's probably nothing, but we fired him after that incident. We waited until closing and it wasn't because of the coffee incident, it was because he was a terrible employee, always late, forgetting to put in orders, and breaking stuff when he was here. He was really quiet, almost too quiet, after your father and I let him go. He just stared at us before taking his tips and leaving. I hadn't even thought about him, but I was just out on the patio delivering bread and saw him drive by our restaurant twice. He's headed back down to your side of the block. It . . . could be nothing, but I wanted to tell you." Her mom's voice shook slightly, telling Julieta that the man must have really bothered her when they let him go because it took a lot to rattle her mother.

"Hold on..." She moved the phone away from her mouth and turned to Ruby. "Will you lock the door and turn the sign to closed?"

Ruby nodded and as she headed for the front, Julieta adjusted the phone. "Thanks for telling me, Mama. I'm closing now and I'll give the name to Lizzy and Ivan."

"When you talk to Lizzy, tell that girl she better bring little Maddox in to see me next week or I'll be calling her mother."

Smiling, she shook her head. Lizzy's new baby was adorable. "I will. And we'll be down to see you soon."

After they disconnected, Julieta couldn't get rid of the nagging sensation in her gut. She knew the name Howell from somewhere. Looking over the file, ice filled her veins as she turned the page. A Leora and Glenn Howell owned a house not far from where the phone had been dumped. A middle-class neighborhood, one of the older ones in Miami so it was established. No Buck Howell though. Still . . . She picked up the file and rounded the counter. She wanted to show it to Ivan. Maybe Lizzy could find out if Buck Howell was related to them.

Before she'd taken two steps an explosion of glass and metal rent the air. Ruby screamed, the fear behind it raking over Julieta's skin. A car surged through one of her front windows, destroying everything in its path.

It swerved in her direction, sending racks of clothes and jewelry flying as it flew straight at her. There was nowhere to go. Her heart jumped in her throat and she dropped the file. She dove over the display, trying to find cover. A mannequin head rolled along the floor as an engine roared loudly.

Her mind whirled as she curled into a ball beneath the display. Ivan, Ruby, she needed to check on them.

The engine still rumbled ominously, but it was idling. She heard a door open and glass crunching as she pushed to her feet.

"Julieta!" Ivan shouted from somewhere to her left. She hoped he wasn't trapped in the security room.

"I'm okay! Ruby, are you all right?" Shaking, she grasped the edge of the display counter and finished getting to her feet. This was too surreal.

As she cleared the counter to stand, all the air rushed from her lungs in a whoosh. The man her mom had been worried about was pointing a gun directly at her, his green eyes wild with rage. He was so close, if he pulled the trigger she'd die in seconds.

"You think you can hide from me?" he snarled.

She just stared at the barrel of the gun, frozen in terror. This maniac had crashed through her store for . . . what? He couldn't think he was getting away which meant he wanted to kill her. She started to shake, a lead ball forming in her stomach. Oh God, why hadn't Ruby answered? Had she been hit by his car? Where was Ivan? Was he okay?

"Answer me!" he screamed, his question jerking her out of her haze.

Her gaze snapped up to his. "I'm not hiding." The words were out before she could think about censoring herself or trying to come up with a good answer. Not that she thought there was actually a good answer for a situation like this. Not when she was staring into the eyes of a man who wanted to kill her.

Moving incredibly fast, he stepped around the counter in two fluid steps and grabbed her by the arm. He shoved the gun into her ribs as he pulled her close. "Damn right you're not hiding. You're mine." His eyes seemed to almost darken as his fingers dug painfully into her upper arm.

She didn't even flinch as a strange numbness invaded her body. She was beyond terrified, but everything around her seemed too surreal, as if she was watching this happen to someone else. Because this couldn't be happening to her. It just couldn't.

He yanked her to the right, around the counter but suddenly jerked to a halt, pulling her in front of him so that her back pressed against his chest. As a shield, she belatedly realized.

At the same time that registered, she saw Ivan standing near one of the pillars that had been saved from this monster's destructive rampage. He had a gun in his hand, pointed in their direction.

"Drop your weapon." His words were quiet as he stared at Buck, but there was a deadly edge to them.

His calmness helped bring her out of her haze. She had the vague thought that she must be going into shock, or maybe she was already in shock. But did people in shock even realize they were in it?

"Julieta, you're going to be okay." Ivan's deep voice punched further through the haze as the man behind her shoved the barrel of the weapon against her head.

She swallowed back the bile in her throat and tried to focus on Ivan.

"Get back or I shoot her right here, right now," the man shouted again even though Ivan was only ten or so feet away from them.

Without the barrier of the counter nothing was in between them. Out of the corner of her eye she saw movement to her left. Ruby. It looked like she was laying on the ground underneath a pile of clothes. If she'd been hit by his car she needed help. Panic suffused her, a jag of adrenaline making her hyperaware of her surroundings.

"You haven't done anything you can't undo right now. There's still time to walk away from this." Ivan's voice was so damn calm. *How* was he so calm?

She wasn't shaking, but she felt as if her insides were. Her heart raced out of control, the beat erratic as blood rushed in her ears. As if she'd split apart from the sheer terror forking through her. She was so damn helpless with no weapons...

Her pepper spray. Ivan had been so insistent she carry it with her *everywhere*.

"Fuck you! This bitch is coming with me and you're going to get out of my way right fucking now!"

Julieta carefully slid her hand into her pocket, her fingers grasping the small weapon tightly. She had no clue how she was moving so smoothly, maybe it was because her whole damn body was so numb.

"All right, I'm moving back." Ivan stepped from the pillar to a fallen rack of corsets. He didn't actually go backward though, more like shifted to the side. It gave Buck a better view of his car though. Maybe it made him feel more in control.

She was vaguely aware of people gathering outside the shop and murmurs of panic, probably because they'd seen the maniac with a gun. It was only a matter of time before the police showed up, before sirens blared in the distance. Deep down Julieta knew it would set this guy off. He was clearly walking a razor's edge. She pulled the pepper spray from her pocket and slid the safety to the side, thankful Ivan had made her practice holding it to get used to the feel of it. She didn't have to look at it to know how to operate it.

The gun moved from her temple and he started waving it at Ivan. "Move on back, keep moving, over to that wall. We're getting out of here and you're not going to do a damn thing to stop me." He smelled like cheap cologne and coffee, the scent invading her nostrils, making her nauseous. He wasn't built like Ivan, but he was taller than her and his grip was incredibly strong.

Raw fear punched through her. Ivan had no protection, nothing to block him from a bullet. No, no, no.

Buck fired, the sound blasting loudly near her ear. She flinched, the echo bringing everything around her into sharp focus. Ivan ducked, his weapon still gripped tightly in his hand as her stalker loosened his hold on her arm.

She didn't even think. Dropping down, she swiveled and brought the pepper spray up. She pressed the trigger, spraying directly at his face.

He screamed and brought one hand up to his face as he started shooting wildly. People outside screamed.

Julieta rolled to the floor, trying to avoid the spray of his madness when suddenly he stopped moving. His body jerked once, twice, and two spots of crimson bloomed on his white T-shirt. Eyes wide, he fell to his knees, his gun-toting hand falling limply to his side as he knelt there, almost suspended in time before he tilted to the side at an awkward angle, his stare on Julieta.

Before she could move, Ivan was suddenly there, holding on to her shoulders and kneeling in front of her. He was mouthing something and it took her a long moment to realize he was asking if she was okay.

There was a ringing in her ear and she felt off balance but she nodded. Or tried to. "Ruby?"

"She's okay. And you're okay." He pulled her into a crushing hug, his big arms wrapping around her so tight he squeezed the air from her lungs.

But she didn't care. She hugged him back, holding onto him for all she was worth.

"I love you," he growled into her hair. His voice shook, his big body trembling as he held her close.

"I love you too," she rasped out against his chest as the sound of sirens finally broke through the air.

CHAPTER THIRTEEN

Tensing, Julieta looked over as the door to her hospital room started to open. She hadn't wanted to come at all, but Detective Duarte had insisted. Ivan had needed to go downtown to fill out a report since he'd shot and killed a man. The detective had wanted to make sure everything was documented and said she needed to come here for a follow up. She'd have come anyway because of Ruby, but she understood Duarte's concerns.

When Ruby had jumped out of the way of that maniac's car, she'd toppled over a couple racks, bruising herself and twisting her ankle. Some glass from one of the displays had shattered over her so she also had a few cuts and nicks on her legs, but everything would heal soon.

Ivan had saved her life and probably Ruby's, but they wanted to be absolutely certain charges weren't brought against him. She'd just been discharged so she'd sent her parents and brothers down to Ruby's room a few minutes ago. She was expecting to see at least one of them back because her family never listened to her.

When Ivan and the detective stepped inside instead, her heart skipped a beat. She moved away from the bench by the window where she'd been checking through her purse to make sure she had everything. Heart beating out of control, she hurried to him. "Ivan. Is everything okay?"

He nodded, a half-smile tugging at his lips as he reached for her. "Yeah."

"Your man is going to be fine," Duarte said, his expression grim. "I just wanted to come down here and reassure you myself."

"Then why do you look like the grim reaper just visited you?"

He paused, his jaw tensing once. "The guy who was after you . . . We got a search warrant for his parent's house and let's just say what we turned up isn't pretty. He's got videos of what he did to former victims. You were incredibly lucky."

Her skin crawled at the news. She was sure the details would come out later but she didn't need them now. And she was pretty sure the detective couldn't tell her how many other women had been victimized so she didn't bother asking. Her heart ached for the families though.

"And the world is a better fucking place without that monster in it," Ivan muttered.

"So trust me, once the media gets a hold of this guy's crimes, the city will want to throw Ivan a parade. Even without the continuing evidence we're gathering, it was a clear case of self-defense against a man with known mental problems stalking you. The State's Attorney won't be making charges against Ivan."

Relief like she'd never experienced before surged through her, soothing the frayed edges of her nerves. "Thank you so much, Detective."

Half-smiling, he nodded. "I got your signed report and I'll be in touch in a couple days to follow up, but you two get some rest."

She'd given her statement to an officer while waiting for a doctor to see her but he'd left her room hours ago. "No problem." She had a lot to deal with like getting her store cleaned up and fixed, dealing with insurance and the potential loss of closing her shop for who knew how long until the repairs were done, but she and Ivan were alive, Ruby was alive and her stalker was dead.

As soon as Duarte left, Julieta turned in Ivan's arms and buried her face against his chest while he pressed his face against the top of her head. "I hate that you had to go down to the police station by yourself," she murmured.

"I wasn't alone." His steady voice was soothing.

Pulling back, she looked up at him. "You weren't?"

"Harrison Caldwell, one of the owners of Red Stone stopped by with one of their attorneys. Even though it wasn't Red Stone business, he was ready to help out if I needed it."

Julieta's eyes widened. "That's pretty impressive."

He just nodded, watching her thoughtfully with those ice blue eyes. "I meant what I said, Julieta. I love you."

She grinned, needing to hear those words. "Good, I did too."

He blinked once, as if he wasn't sure he'd heard her right.

"That wasn't a confession based on intense circumstances or whatever, I know how I feel. I love you, Ivan. I know we've got a lot to learn about each other and I'm excited about that."

He let out a slow breath and leaned down, giving her time to pull back. She nearly snorted at the thought. As if she could ever pull back from this man. When he just brushed his lips over hers then lifted his head she had to bite back a groan. But now wasn't the time to start something they couldn't finish. And she knew he had to be just as exhausted as she was. "Want to go see Ruby then get out of here? I don't think they're keeping her overnight so she might be checking out soon too."

"Sounds good to me. Then we're getting you home and to bed. You need rest," he murmured.

She needed more than rest, but she just smiled and nodded. She'd show him exactly what she needed soon enough.

* * *

Julieta looked at herself in her bathroom mirror one last time before turning away and heading for the door. After visiting with Ruby last night for a couple hours and waiting for her to get discharged, they'd all left the hospital together. Then Julieta and Ivan had returned to his place and picked up most of her things. She'd been determined to sleep in her own house even if it was well after midnight by the time they'd gotten here.

Because she wasn't letting that psycho Buck steal any more of her life from her. She was reclaiming her home, including her bedroom.

Unfortunately all Ivan had wanted to do was sleep when they got back. She was certain if she'd pushed him he would have been up for more but he'd looked so exhausted and the truth was, by the time they'd finally made it back, she'd been ready to crash too. Now that she'd gotten some rest she was wired and ready for Ivan.

About ten minutes ago Ivan had gotten out of bed so she'd pretended to be asleep. It was only a little after six, but from her past week's experience with him she'd come to realize that he was an early riser. Even more so than her.

When he came back upstairs she planned to surprise him. Because she wasn't waiting any longer for a taste of him. He'd been more than willing to sleep in the same bed with her the last week and they'd definitely gotten physical but she wanted everything from him, wanted to cement the bond that had blossomed between them.

As she opened the bathroom door, she jerked to a halt. She hadn't expected him upstairs yet but Ivan stood in the doorway of her room, shirtless and gorgeous, two coffee cups in hand. His blue eyes widened and he sucked in a sharp breath as his gaze tracked her from head to toe.

She was wearing what he called her red fuck-me heels and nothing else. "Put the coffee down and get on the bed," she said in the most demanding voice she could muster. Her voice shook a little, but from pure desire.

He paused, his gaze riveted to hers, and she guessed he was fighting that dominant streak of his. He liked to be in control, which was fine with her most of the time, at least in the bedroom. But now it was her turn.

His jaw tightened as he set the mugs on the nearest dresser. When he turned back to her, his eyes were molten with need. Her own gaze trailed down to the bulge hidden behind his boxer briefs. She knew from this past week just how impressive he was. But he'd only let her stroke him with her hands. Now, she was going to kiss and lick him like she'd been fantasizing about. There wasn't any reason for him to hold back anymore.

Watching her, he hooked his fingers on the elastic of his briefs and slid them down his muscular legs. Just like every other time she'd seen him, her mouth practically watered as she drank in all of him.

Broad shoulders, a trim waist, thighs so muscular she wanted to trace her fingers over every striation, then follow up with her tongue. When she imagined what a Viking must have looked like, he was it. All sexy blond god with a perfect physique.

As he stepped out of the briefs, instead of heading for the bed, he stalked straight toward her, like a predator moving in on his prey.

"Bed." Hand on one hip, she pointed at the bed with her other, trying to be commanding but utterly failed when he reached her.

Without saying a word he buried his fingers in her hair, cupping the back of her head tight as his mouth descended on hers. There was no build up, just a serious claiming as he wrapped his free hand around her, pressing her flush against him.

Not that she needed the direction. Her nipples beaded tight as he bent over her, his chest rubbing hers. She arched her back, increasing the friction as she clutched onto his shoulders. When he groaned into her mouth, his big body trembling, her inner walls contracted at the sound.

Hearing him so affected by her lit her up, the need sparking through her like an out of control wildfire. Suddenly his hands were on her hips, lifting her up. She knew what he wanted and wrapped her legs around him as he walked them to the bed.

Still eating at her mouth like a man possessed, he splayed her out under him, his cock resting against her abdomen as she dug her heels into his ass. He groaned even louder before tearing his head back. Breathing hard, his chest rising and falling against hers as he stared down at her, she could see how close he was to losing control. She couldn't wait.

"I didn't want to rush you . . . You're sure?" His words were choppy, further proof of his lack of control.

She slowly stroked her fingers up and down his back, savoring the way his muscles flexed under her touch. "I want to take you inside me, to come around your cock, to feel you coming in me." She'd never been into dirty talk in the bedroom before, but she wanted Ivan to know exactly what she wanted. She was tired of waiting for him, for this, to finally be completely possessed by this wonderful man.

His hips rolled against her, his hard length pressing into her abdomen at her words. His pupils dilated, his breathing even more ragged as he swallowed hard, the sound almost over pronounced in the room. Taking her by surprise, he rolled them over, letting her straddle him. They'd already talked about protection earlier this week and since she was on the pill and they'd both been tested there was no need for condoms. She couldn't wait to feel him inside her. Their bodies were almost perfectly positioned.

Right now she was under no illusion that she was in control, but she liked being on top, having this man under her. Straddling him, she pushed up against his chest, shimmying up his body so that she stroked her wet lips over his hard length.

His eyes grew heavy-lidded as he watched her, his fingers flexing tight against her hips before he let go. "Sit on my face."

The bold words made her inner walls tighten, clenching with the need to be filled. By him. She wanted to take him into her mouth then slide on to him, but . . . The hungry look on Ivan's face had her doing exactly what he said.

Even though it made her feel vulnerable to be in such an intimate position with him, she climbed up his body and lowered herself onto his face. Growling, he reached up and wrapped his fingers onto her thighs, holding her tight and refusing to let her close her legs as he dipped his tongue inside her. It should be illegal how talented he was with his tongue. An uncontrollable shudder skittered through her as she let out a soft moan.

"Touch yourself," he ordered, his words strangled before he swiped his tongue along her wet slit.

She tried to move, but he held her in position as he stroked her. Even though she was on top, he was still in complete control, his wicked tongue teasing as she reached up to cup her breasts.

She'd never been so open with her past lovers and had often felt rushed to orgasm, sometimes even faking it. Her toys had always been a sure thing. And she'd come to find out that so was Ivan. The past week she'd never felt remotely rushed, not with Ivan's attention so focused, his determination to make her climax to the point where he put her totally first an incredible turn on. She found herself coming easier and easier with him, her body attuned to him.

Which was why it was no surprise when he focused on her clit with that maddeningly perfect pressure she could feel the buildup start. It stunned her how quickly he'd learned her body. As she gently held her breasts, rubbing over her nipples with her thumbs, she started to tremble. But she didn't want to come against his mouth this time.

Even though it was almost painful to do so, she let her hands fall. "Ivan, stop."

His fingers loosened on her thighs, his gaze meeting hers as she looked down at him. "What's wrong? You're close, I can feel it." The harshly spoken words were almost an accusation.

She shook her head and started moving down the length of his body, keeping him straddled underneath her as she went. "I'm not coming against your mouth." Leaning down, she brushed her lips over his small, flat brown nipple before gently pressing her teeth around the small nub.

He slid his fingers through her hair, holding onto her head with one hand and her shoulder with the other. "What are you doing?" A quiet question, the tension in his voice making her smile as she moved lower, kissing a path along the hard ridges of his abdomen.

"Taking what I want," she whispered, reaching his hard length. Before taking it in her mouth, she lightly swiped her tongue across the head.

His hips jerked, his cock bobbing against his stomach as he let out a dirty curse. His words made her smile and she did it again, holding onto his erection at the base to hold him in place. She flicked her tongue over him, barely grazing him, then gently blew on him.

"Your mouth," he groaned, the words sounding as if they were torn from his throat.

With her other hand, she reached between them and cupped his balls. When she tugged on them, he surged into her mouth. Taking him as deep as she could, she moaned, knowing he'd love the vibration against his thick length.

"Jules," he said her name like a prayer, her nickname falling from his lips so easily. She loved hearing it, loved everything she'd learned about this man.

Moving slowly, she took her time as she drew him as deep as she could before releasing him. Over and over, she teased him until he made a strangled sound and grabbed her shoulders, pulling her up.

Before she could ask what he was doing, he pulled her up then flipped her under him. Oh yeah, he wanted to be in control, and she was ready to give him the reins. He kept his gaze pinned to hers as he reached between their bodies.

Cupping her mound, he shuddered when he slid a finger inside her. "So wet," he murmured as he withdrew it. Without using his hand as a guide, he positioned his hard length between her slick lips.

Ivan watched her closely as he placed his hands on either side of her head, keeping most of his weight off her. It was the most erotic sensation to have his cock pressing at her entrance but not have his hands on her.

She had no such control. Stroking her fingers up his abdomen, chest, then back down again, she grabbed onto his waist, digging her fingers into his hard body as she arched into him. The spiciness that was partly from the body wash he used and mostly just his natural scent wrapped around her like a warm embrace. She loved everything about him and wanted to bury her face against his neck and just breathe him in.

Her body opened to him as he surged forward with a groan. His mouth captured hers, his cock sliding into her in one long thrust. She gasped into his kiss as he filled her completely. Her body stretched and molded around him, taking all he had to give.

It didn't matter that she'd been primed for him, it had still been a long time and he was thick. Almost immediately her inner walls started convulsing around him, little ripples of her impending orgasm starting. Oh yeah, it wasn't going to take her long at all.

As if he'd read her mind, he reached between them. He stayed buried inside her, barely moving as he tweaked her clit. Just like that, her climax started, a sharp punch of pleasure ricocheting to all her nerve endings. Reading her perfectly, he increased his pressure between her thighs, rubbing against her sensitive bundle of nerves with his thumb as he began moving.

The additional friction was too much, sending her into erotic overdrive. Her orgasm increased, cresting into so much pleasure she couldn't think straight as her head fell back from his. Even kissing took too much focus. Eyes closed, she arched into him, clutching at his shoulders as he pounded into her, his thrusts erratic as she shouted her release.

Just as quickly, he fell over that edge with her, groaning her name like a prayer as he thrust, over and over, his thickness the most wonderful feeling she'd ever experienced. As her orgasm started to ebb she managed to open her eyes a fraction, watching as Ivan stared down at her, pure ecstasy on his face as he lost himself inside her.

It was impossible to look away from the stark beauty of his face as he was at his most vulnerable. She wasn't sure how much time passed but eventually his thrusts slowed, his release warm inside her.

He cupped her cheek with his calloused palm, gently stroking over her skin with his thumb. "I'm grateful every fucking day that I met you. I can't imagine my life without you in it."

She sucked in a breath at his words, the sincerity in them touching her bone-deep. He might have told her that he loved her, but this felt like more, a deeper confession somehow. The truth was, she couldn't imagine her life without him in it either.

Reaching around him, she hugged him close, loving the skin to skin contact. "Good, because I'm not going anywhere." She didn't know what the future held for them but she knew what she wanted with him; the whole package.

EPILOGUE

Two and a half months later

"Why are you looking at me like that?" Julieta murmured, going up on her toes to kiss Ivan.

"Like what?" Probably like he wanted to devour her right there—because he did. But getting naked and having his way with her on one of the lounge chairs next to her parents' pool at their big New Year's party would be inappropriate. And get him an ass kicking by her brothers—and her cousins.

"You know what." Her voice was a seductive whisper as she leaned into him.

They were surrounded by about fifty people, mostly her family, but some friends as well, for the big party. For the past couple months they'd been practically living together, switching back and forth between both their places. But he wanted so much more from her.

He wanted forever. Damn it, he'd planned to wait until midnight and do a big romantic gesture, but Jules staring at him with those big brown eyes in that formfitting gold dress that wrapped around her delicious body like a second skin—he couldn't stand it anymore. He needed his ring on her finger and he didn't care how caveman that made him. He wanted the entire world to know she was his. Hell, he wanted her to know how much she meant to him.

At one time the thought of marriage would have terrified him but the thought of not having Julieta in his life was far more terrifying. Without pause he went down on one knee, taking her left hand in his. Out of respect he'd already talked to her parents to let them know his intentions. Technically he'd asked for permission but the truth was, if they'd said no, he'd have asked her to marry him anyway. Julieta was his.

Her pretty lips parted in surprise as she stared at him, wide-eyed. She opened her mouth as if to say something, but no words came out.

Pulling the small box from his pants' pocket, he wasn't surprised that his hands were rock steady. He'd never been more sure of anything in his life. Around them he was vaguely aware of everyone going silent and the sound of the music dimming, but all his focus was on the woman he loved more than anything.

He held the blue box in his hand, but still hadn't opened it. "I wanted to wait until midnight—"

"Yes!" she shouted, taking him by surprise.

Relief slammed into him, the small insecure part of him that had been worried she'd say no, soothed in the best way possible. His mouth curved into a grin. "I don't think I asked a question yet," he murmured low enough for only her to hear.

In response she held out her hand expectantly, her grin wicked and her eyes shimmering with tears. "You better put that ring on my finger right now, Mr. Mitchell."

At that, his cock hardened instantly. She only ever called him Mr. Mitchell playfully in the bedroom. Thankfully his bent leg hid his response from their onlookers. Without waiting another second, he opened the box and slid the marquis cut diamond onto her finger. Oh yeah, he loved the way it looked.

She let out a gasp at the sight of the ring before she bent and threw her arms around his neck, practically tackling him. Catching her in his arms, he stood, pulling her with him as he captured her mouth with his. She tasted sweet, like the wine she'd been drinking earlier. Cheers and the sound of champagne bottles popping sounded around them, but he had eyes only for her.

Though it pained him to pull away, he did, looking down into the eyes of the woman he planned to spend the rest of his life with, to have children with. Growing up as an only child and with a father who was gone all the time, he'd craved having a family of his own his whole life, even if he'd never admitted it to himself. "I love you."

"I love you too." Her voice was a scratchy whisper, the joy and love in her eyes shining through as they were bombarded by people wishing them congratulations. Glasses of champagne were pushed into their hands and her brothers immediately started giving toasts, mostly threatening to kick his ass if he ever hurt their sister.

Ivan wrapped an arm around Julieta's shoulders and pulled her in tight to his side. That was one thing he'd never do. Julieta was the best thing that had ever happened to him and he couldn't wait to start their lives together.

Thank you for reading Under His Protection. I really hope you enjoyed it and that you'll consider leaving a review at one of your favorite online retailers. It's a great way to help other readers discover new books.

If you liked Under His Protection and would like to read more, turn the page for a sneak peek of Bound to Danger, the second book in my Deadly Ops series. And if you don't want to miss any future releases, please feel free to join my newsletter. I only send out a newsletter for new releases or sales news. Find the signup link on my website: http://www.katiereus.com

BOUND TO DANGER

Deadly Ops Series
Copyright © 2014 Katie Reus

Forcing her body to obey her when all she wanted
to do was curl into a ball and cry until she passed out,
she got up. Cool air rushed over her exposed back and
backside as her feet hit the chilly linoleum floor. She
wasn't wearing any panties and the hospital gown
wasn't covering much of her. She didn't care.

Right now she didn't care about much at all.

Sometime when she'd been asleep her dirty, rumpled gown had been removed from the room. And
someone had left a small bag of clothes on the bench
by the window. No doubt Nash had brought her something to wear. He'd been in to see her a few times, but
she'd asked him to leave each time. She felt like a
complete bitch because she knew he just wanted to
help, but she didn't care. Nothing could help, and being alone with her pain was the only way she could
cope right now.

Feeling as if she were a hundred years old, she'd
started unzipping the small brown leather bag when
the door opened. As she turned to look over her shoulder, she found Nash, a uniformed police officer, and
another really tall, thuggish-looking man entering.

Her eyes widened in recognition. The tattoos were
new, but the *thug* was Cade O'Reilly. He'd served in
the Marines with her brother. They'd been best friends
and her brother, Riel, named after her father, had even
brought him home a few times. But that was years ago.
Eight to be exact. It was hard to forget the man who'd
completely cut her out of his life after her brother died,
as if she meant nothing to him.

Cade towered over Nash—who was pretty tall himself—and had a sleeve of tattoos on one arm and a couple on the other. His jet-black hair was almost shaved, the skull trim close to his head, just like the last time she'd seen him. He was . . . intimidating. Always had been. And startlingly handsome in that badboy way she was sure had made plenty of women . . . Yeah, she wasn't even going there.

She swiveled quickly, putting her back to the window so she wasn't flashing them. Reaching around to her back, she clasped the hospital gown together. "You can't knock?" she practically shouted, her voice raspy from crying, not sure whom she was directing the question to.

"I told them you weren't to be bothered, but—"

The police officer cut Nash off, his gaze kind but direct. "Ms. Cervantes, this man is from the NSA and needs to ask you some questions. As soon as you're done, the doctors will release you."

"I know who he is." She bit the words out angrily, earning a surprised look from Nash and a controlled look from Cade.

She might know Cade, or she had at one time, but she hadn't known he worked for the NSA. After her brother's death he'd stopped communicating with her. Her brother had brought him home during one of their short leaves, and she and Cade had become friends. *Good friends.* They'd e-mailed all the time, for almost a year straight. Right near the end of their long correspondence, things had shifted between them, had been heading into more than friendly territory. Then after Riel died, it was as if Cade had too. It had cut her so deep to lose him on top of her brother. And now he showed up in the hospital room after her mom's death and wanted to talk to her? Hell no.

She'd been harassing the nurses to find a doctor who would discharge her, and now she knew why they'd been putting her off. They'd done a dozen tests and she didn't have a brain injury. She wasn't exhibiting any signs of having a concussion except for the memory loss, but the doctors were convinced that this was because of shock and trauma at what she'd apparently witnessed.

Nash started to argue, but the cop hauled him away, talking in low undertones, shutting the door behind them. Leaving her alone with this giant of a man.

Feeling raw and vulnerable, Maria wrapped her arms around herself. The sun had almost set, so even standing by the window didn't warm her up. She just felt so damn cold. Because of the room and probably grief. And now to be faced with a dark reminder of her past was too much.

ACKNOWLEDGMENTS

A great big thank you to Kari Walker for her insight with this book (as always)! I also owe thanks to Joan Turner for her copy editing skills and Jaycee with Sweet 'N Spicy Designs for the beautiful cover. For my readers, the ninth book in the Red Stone Security series is here because of you. Thank you for reading this series. Every day I'm humbled that you love this world as much as me. I wouldn't get to write so much without a supportive husband so as always, thank you. Last but not least, I'm thankful to God.

COMPLETE BOOKLIST

Red Stone Security Series
No One to Trust
Danger Next Door
Fatal Deception
Miami, Mistletoe & Murder
His to Protect
Breaking Her Rules
Protecting His Witness
Sinful Seduction
Under His Protection

The Serafina: Sin City Series
First Surrender
Sensual Surrender
Sweetest Surrender

Deadly Ops Series
Targeted
Bound to Danger

Non-series Romantic Suspense
Running From the Past
Everything to Lose

Dangerous Deception
Dangerous Secrets
Killer Secrets
Deadly Obsession
Danger in Paradise
His Secret Past

Paranormal Romance
Destined Mate
Protector's Mate
A Jaguar's Kiss
Tempting the Jaguar
Enemy Mine
Heart of the Jaguar

Moon Shifter Series
Alpha Instinct
Lover's Instinct (novella)
Primal Possession
Mating Instinct
His Untamed Desire (novella)
Avenger's Heat
Hunter Reborn

Darkness Series
Darkness Awakened
Taste of Darkness

ABOUT THE AUTHOR

Katie Reus is the *New York Times* and *USA Today* bestselling author of the Red Stone Security series, the Moon Shifter series and the Deadly Ops series. She fell in love with romance at a young age thanks to books she pilfered from her mom's stash. Years later she loves reading romance almost as much as she loves writing it.

However, she didn't always know she wanted to be a writer. After changing majors many times, she finally graduated summa cum laude with a degree in psychology. Not long after that she discovered a new love. Writing. She now spends her days writing dark paranormal romance and sexy romantic suspense. For more information on Katie please visit her website: www.katiereus.com. Also find her on twitter @katiereus or visit her on facebook at: www.facebook.com/katiereusauthor.

Printed in Great Britain
by Amazon.co.uk, Ltd.,
Marston Gate.